Also by Shona Bradbury

An Original Roswell (2014)

Gesticulations (2016)

Learn more at shonabradbury.com.

Changing Realms

A Novella

by Shona Bradbury

For Michael and Morgan.
We are whole in this realm.

PROLOGUE

Two years ago...

PSYCHIATRIC ASSESSMENT
From the office of Dr. Philip Sawyer

Date of Consultation: JULY 23, 2013
Consulting Physician: Dr. Philip Sawyer, M.D.
Patient: Elizabeth Percy
Identification: Patient is an 18-year-old female.
Presenting Complaint(s): Schizophrenia presenting with delusional behavior. Patient claims to be symptom free for one year.
History of Present Illness: Patient was orphaned at birth, mother died and father missing. She was subsequently placed in foster care. Her numerous foster parents reported delusional behavior during adolescence. Patient was admitted to Marlowe Psychiatric Hospital in Sacramento, CA at age seven presenting with symptoms of schizophrenia. As a child, patient described the delusions as living two lives. For ten years, under the care of Dr. Archer Ripley, the patient recounted the daily happenings of a second life in rural England in the mid 1500s. Records show the patient stated she was "transported" to the other life during her sleep each night. At age 18, the patient was no longer considered a ward of the state of California and was released for out-patient care once per week. As she is no longer showing symptoms of schizophrenia, she does not meet criteria for further state funded mental health institutionalization. Her case worker applied for and was

granted an extension of her psychotherapy treatment on an out-patient basis not to expire before her 21st birthday.

Current Medications: 12.5 mg fluphenazine decanoate injections (have been weaning the patient off for the past six months)

Personal History: Patient is single with no children. Patient has obtained employment at a local grocery/retail store.

Family History: Unknown. Mother deceased. Father missing.

Mental Status Examination: During our first visit, patient sat neatly with good posture. She spoke with precision and good manners. She was guarded and did not offer any information that wasn't specifically asked. She denies experiencing any delusions for the past year. She tensed when I referenced the delusions as possible dreams. Her expression leads me to believe that she views my reference to her delusions as dreams to be an insult. The patient may have been prematurely diagnosed with schizophrenia at an early age, although delusional behavior may lead to full on schizophrenia at some point in her life. Based on her body language, I believe she may still have the delusions, but is hiding her symptoms to avoid being re-institutionalized. Patient also regularly incorporates the use of medieval jargon in her conversational vocabulary. Her dialect is partially consistent with the era of delusions.

Laboratory Data: Blood work shows no signs of recreational drug use. Only small amounts of fluphenazine decanoate remain.

Diagnosis:

Axis I: Possible Delusional Disorder, Schizophrenia

Axis II: Deferred, personality disorder to be determined

Axis III: No physical or neurological abnormalities present in PET, MRI, or CT scans.

Axis IV: Stress factors: New job, new housing

Axis V: Global Assessment of Functioning rated at 51-60 upon initial consultation; moderate symptoms

Recommendation and Plan: The patient has agreed to the mandatory visits for one hour weekly to discuss her post-institutionalization transition. We will concentrate on discussions about her employment and social interactions. We will work to build a relationship of trust with the patient. A full drug-free recovery of schizophrenia is rare, but not unheard of. Patient may have been misdiagnosed or else may be masking her symptoms.

1

TUESDAY, AUGUST 4, 2015 MARYSVILLE, CA

It was morning. Liz knew this without opening her eyes by the reddish orange glow that the sun was pushing through her closed lids. She also knew which world she awoke in by the stench of the city. The pollution crept through the small window she had left slightly open the last night she fell asleep here. She began to cry and refused to open her eyes.

If I don't open my eyes, then I'm not here yet.

That wasn't true. Liz knew the transformation was instant. Thinking of that, she cried a little longer. Finally, she opened her eyes. She wiped away the blurriness of her tears. As the tiny bedroom of her efficiency apartment came into view, she grimaced.

At least it is cheap.

She pulled back the thin coverlet and took a moment to stare at the pink cotton pajama pants she had put on two days ago. For all others in this realm, it had only been last night, but for her it felt longer. It felt as if two days had passed. This nightwear was so unlike one of the satin nightgowns she would have worn the night before. She would awake wearing something of that nature the next time. She had to get through today first.

She got out of bed and took the two strides necessary to enter the adjoining bathroom. She glimpsed herself in the mirror. Sometimes, she was startled by her own appearance. Especially in this world. Her hair was shorter and darker here. Mirrors weren't especially prevalent in the other realm, nor did they provide such a clear translation of a person's image. She opened the mirrored cabinet and looked inside. Many boxes of antihistamines and bottles of GABA were displayed before her. She reached for a bottle of melatonin and took a dose.

She took a long, hot shower. She enjoyed the showers of this world very much. The modern plumbing was the only thing she missed when she was on the other side. As much as she relished the powerful sting of this hot shower, she would gladly trade it for an uninterrupted lifetime of tepid baths.

After she dressed, she took the additional five strides necessary to reach her small kitchenette. She popped a decaffeinated pod into her single serve coffee maker. It had been purchased at very little cost from the place she worked. With her meager income, she kept an eye on items that were returned and placed on clearance. Even then, she could only afford such extravagance when combined with her store discount. She took an individually packaged yogurt cup from the refrigerator and a spoon from the cutlery drawer, then sat at the small table which functioned both as a dining area and computer desk. She checked the calendar. This was the last week of the month. After she opened up her laptop, which had also been a discounted clearance purchase from her place of employment, she logged into her financial accounts and authorized payments for her rent and utilities, which were due at the beginning of the coming month. She marveled at the convenience and autonomy of online bill paying.

It was a Tuesday. She would have to go to work. She had a full-time job in this world. The job was nothing special, but it paid the bills. She was a cashier at a discount superstore. It was "super" because it sold a little bit of everything. A customer could complete one-stop shopping if he or she needed a computer, a wedding ring and a dozen eggs. She was a full-time employee which provided healthcare benefits as well. Healthcare benefits were important in this world.

Because it was Tuesday, she would have an appointment with Dr. Philip Sawyer as well. She thought about what she would tell him this week. Should she go into detail about the differences in sleepwear that she owns in each realm? She thought not. Not unless she wanted to partake of Marlowe Psychiatric Hospital inpatient services again. She did not.

For three years, she had worked hard to appear normal during her visits, denying her alternate life. She was unsure why Dr. Sawyer continued their weekly visits. She suspected he did not believe her. Liz admitted to herself she wasn't a very good liar. Still, he had no evidence of her other life. He could petition the court to release her from mandatory counseling if he wanted to. She continued the appointments without formal complaint for fear of being committed to a mental institution again.

She finished her breakfast and packed a lunch to take along. She gathered up a few personal belongings and stepped outside. Her apartment was on the second floor. She scanned the courtyard. All the apartments in the complex faced inward toward the gardens. It was lovely. The manager who lived onsite, Evelyn, had a proper gift for landscaping. The gardens resembled a tropical resort. It was a delightful view to behold from the second floor landing.

As she turned back to her door to lock the dead bolt, she saw her neighbor, Noah, also exiting his apartment. He lived directly across from her. She knew little about Noah. They appeared to be the same age. She never asked where he worked or where he was from. He, on the other hand, pestered her incessantly. Sometimes, she didn't know how to answer him. *Where are you from? What are your hobbies? Where do you go in your spare time?* It took great effort on her part to deliver and remember her answers.

"Hi, Liz!" he shouted across the courtyard. He jogged over to meet her at the top of the exit stairwell, which was on her side of the complex.

"Good morrow, Noah," she responded.

"Are you coming to Evelyn's barbecue tonight?" he asked. On Tuesday nights, the building manager lit the grill in the courtyard. Neighbors convened as they took turns cooking their meat and vegetables on the grill. People also brought down their choice of beverage in small coolers. The gatherings seemed to be very pleasant and were never rowdy.

"No, I don't think…"

"Come on! You can come just this once. If you don't

like it, then I will never ask again."

"OK, just this once. But I cannot stay the whole time. I need to get to bed early tonight."

"Deal." He smiled and parted ways toward his car.

Liz walked over to her car. It was unlocked, which was not how she left it. As she slid into the driver's side, she noticed, once again, her stereo was gone. Thieves were brazen in this area. She parked her car in the well-lit apartment lot. Someone in an apartment on the first floor looking out their lot-facing window would have been able to witness the theft. This was the third time it had happened to her. She sighed and decided that replacing the unit would be futile. Even with her store discount, replacement of the stereo regularly was not in her budget. Reporting the robbery to the police would also be useless. Her car was thirty years old. Popping the locks took very little effort with a clothes hanger.

Liz drove to work and parked in the employee lot. She locked the car out of habit. She used her access card to enter the store from the back. After dropping her lunch into the break room refrigerator, she used the same card swipe to clock in. She walked to her manager's office to retrieve her cashier tray. Daphne looked up from her computer screen when Liz knocked at the door.

"Good morning, Liz," Daphne flashed a genuine smile. Liz was her favorite employee because she was always punctual, followed the rules, was pleasant to the customers and never had a light drawer.

"Hello Daphne," Liz smiled back at her. Daphne turned to hand Liz her cashier tray for the day.

"Liz, could you have your lunch break with me today?"

"Why?"

"There is something I would like to discuss with you," Daphne smiled again.

"Have I done something wrong?" Liz asked.

"Not at all," Daphne smiled again.

"OK, I will come see you during my break today," Liz took the offered tray. "Which register am I at?"

"Number 10. See you at lunch."

"Sounds good."

Liz left the office feeling a little curious. The rest of her morning was uneventful. Shoppers were sparse and orderly for a change. Liz was pleasant to all who used her shopping lane. She assisted when help was sought. She guided when product navigation was asked. She smiled, scanned and bagged for four hours.

When her break time neared, she flashed the light for aisle 10 to signal her last customer. She used her two-way radio to contact Daphne and let her know she was on her way to the break room. She stopped by the refrigerator to pick up her lunch bag. Daphne was there to get her lunch bag as well. The two women headed to Daphne's office. Liz took a seat and smiled at Daphne. Daphne pushed her monitor to the side to give Liz room on the desktop surface to use as a tabletop for her lunch. They both emptied their lunch bags on the desk.

"Thanks for spending this time with me today. I wanted to let you know that I spoke with Vanessa at headquarters yesterday."

Liz arched an eyebrow. She wondered what this conversation had to do with her.

"We would like to offer you an assistant manager position here at the store," Daphne beamed.

"Really?" Liz was surprised. She hadn't been seeking a promotion. She was comfortable with the status quo. Her current wage covered her simple needs. The small amount of responsibility in her current position suited her as well. She saved her ambition for the other realm.

"Yes, we would send you to Sacramento for manager training next month. The wage increase would kick in at that time. It is still an hourly rate, but $10 more an hour than you are presently making."

"Wow, thank you for the offer," Liz said. "Would this promotion change my schedule?"

"Yes, it would. As a new assistant manager, you would cover the evening hours and continue to work some weekends."

Liz winced internally, but tried not to let it show. Evening work was something that she could not commit to without assessing the impact on her other schedule.

"Could I have some time to think about it?"

"Of course," Daphne responded, but her expression clearly revealed her confusion. She had expected Liz to jump at the chance or show a bit of enthusiasm. She knew Liz had not gone to college, nor had she mentioned any other career plans for the future. Liz had worked full time for the store for two years. She started right after her release from Marlowe. Daphne had no privilege to the records of Liz's time at the psychiatric hospital.

Liz began to gather up her lunch to retreat to the break room.

"No, please stay," Daphne insisted. "We can chat."

Liz smiled and released her food items back to the desk.

"Tomorrow starts your weekend. Do you have any plans?" Daphne asked. Working in retail, it was common for a cashier's 'weekend' to fall in the middle of the week. Liz's schedule allowed Wednesdays and Thursdays to be free.

"No, nothing special. I usually do some shopping and laundry."

"I always imagine you young folks having a line of parties and dates on your weekends," Daphne smiled. She herself wasn't 'old' by any means. Liz guessed her to be in her mid to late twenties.

"My apartment complex is holding a potluck barbecue tonight," Liz offered. "It will be my first time attending. It is a 'bring your own meat and drink' type of event."

"Oh, that sounds fun," Daphne smiled. "What will you be bringing?"

"I don't know. I thought I would stop by the butcher's department on my way out to see if anything looked good."

"I recommend a chicken breast. You can marinate it and throw it on a roll to eat as a sandwich while you mingle. And stop by the bakery. This morning I saw Marge put out some delicious macaroons that you can share."

"Thanks for the tip," Liz smiled. She finished her lunch. "I should get back to my station."

"Enjoy your weekend. We can talk some more on Friday morning when you come in."

"Thank you, again," Liz said. Once she was out of earshot from Daphne's office, she exhaled a huge breath. She wondered how she was going to turn down the opportunity. She would need to think of a less crazy-sounding reason than she could presently provide. And what would happen after she declined? Would she be able to keep her current cashier position? She decided to check the time zone schedule when she got home that evening to see if she could make a promotion work. After she put her empty lunch bag in her locker, she returned to checkout aisle 10. She flipped on the light to signal that the lane was open for customers.

Another four hours of work and it was time to clock out. The shift change was smooth that night. Liz stopped by the grocery department and picked up a chicken breast, the macaroons, a dinner roll, and some teriyaki sauce on her way out. She took her items home and quickly set the chicken to marinate in the refrigerator. She had twenty minutes to get to her appointment with Dr. Philip Sawyer.

IT ONLY TOOK HER FIFTEEN minutes to get to his office. She signed in with his receptionist. Her name was Tina, and she was always kind to Liz. Liz took the seat in the hallway outside Dr. Sawyer's office. She heard the telltale sound of his current patient leaving through the unseen exit used for discretion. Dr. Sawyer opened his primary door a few minutes later. He was a good-looking man with dark brown hair and light brown eyes. Liz thought his features showed a Greek descent, but it was harder to distinguish a person's origin in this future world. She considered it to be a tribute to the 460 years of melting pot experience the New World gained since she left the other realm that morning. She had never asked Dr. Sawyer's age, but she guessed he was in his late thirties or early forties.

"Liz, come on in," he said.

She entered the room and sat in an oversized leather upholstered chair in front of his desk. There were two chairs facing each other. Sometimes, Dr. Sawyer sat in the other chair. Today, he took his seat behind the desk. He opened her considerable folder and added a page for today's session notes. As a tribute to his efficiency, the page had questions already printed as a worksheet to guide their session. He handwrote the day's date in the top right corner.

"How are you?" he asked.

"Good," she lied. *This world depresses me, but you probably know that, or we wouldn't still be having sessions.*

He looked at the prepared questions, then back at her. He then thumbed through a few other recent pages in the folder.

"Ahh, here it is. Your drug screen came back negative for any illegal substances."

"You sound surprised," she challenged.

"Not at all," he smiled at her and went back to his folder and made a note. "Let's get started with the usual questions. First, have you had any more dreams of the other life?"

"No." Her eyes narrowed. *They aren't dreams.*

"OK," he gave her a pensive look. Then he returned to his prepared questionnaire and made a note. "What do you dream about?"

"Cats, spaceships, and Zac Efron," she lied. "Not all together at once. Well, sometimes," she smiled. He made a note.

"How is your job?" he asked.

"Good," she didn't tell him about the offer of promotion.

"Have you thought about college?" he asked. "It's never too late."

"No," she didn't have to lie to answer that. She would have to take night courses in order to keep her job. Her evenings needed to remain free. "I'm happy with how things are now. My job pays for my apartment and my car." He made a note.

"Have you made any new friends?" he asked.

"Yes," she answered.

He looked up in surprise.

"I'm going to a barbecue tonight with my friend, Noah," she continued.

"Noah?"

"Yes, he is my neighbor," she answered.

"Is it a date?" he asked.

"Of course not," she sputtered too quickly. *Shit, shit, shit!*

"Why is that such a farfetched question?" he asked. He looked at her intently for an answer.

"I don't know," she answered, gaining her composure. "I feel 'twould be in bad form to become involved with someone who lives in the same building." *And I could never be unfaithful to Leonardo, but I can't tell him about Leonardo.* Instead, she continued, "What if it didn't work out? Then I would still have to see him every day."

"That is very mature thinking," he smiled.

Relief spread over her face. Dr. Sawyer made another note.

"It has been three years since you have had the dreams

and two years since our first visit," he stated. "In this time, you have demonstrated responsibility through steady employment and paying your rent and utilities on time. I am pleased that you are socializing with your neighbors. Please continue to provide the monthly urine sample to the clinic." He made a few more notes on the prepared document. "Is there anything you would like to talk about today?"

"Nope."

"This was a quick visit. Next week, we can discuss decreasing the frequency of your visits."

"'Tis good news, indeed." Her smile was the most genuine it had been during all of her previous visits.

"I look forward to hearing about the barbecue during our next visit." He made one last session note and laid down his pen.

"Speaking of which, unless I am to kiss the hare's foot, I must be on my way." she stood and made her way to the discreet exit.

"No, you don't want to be late for dinner," he smiled, as he had learned a fair amount of medieval slang without letting on over the past two years.

Dr. Sawyer watched Liz leave. It would be another thirty minutes before his next appointment. He dialed the number for Marlowe Psychiatric Hospital.

"Thank you for calling Marlowe Psychiatric Hospital. How may I direct your call?" A soft-spoken young man answered the phone.

"Hello, I would like to speak with Dr. Archer Ripley, please. Tell him Dr. Philip Sawyer is calling."

"I'm sorry, sir, but Dr. Ripley is in session right now. May I take a message?" the young man responded.

"Yes, tell him I would like to speak with him again regarding Elizabeth Percy. Thank you so much." Philip gave the young man his contact information.

Philip ended the call and looked at his computer screen. He pulled up a video of a session Liz had with Dr. Ripley when she was thirteen years old. After a few minutes, he turned it off and shook his head. He looked at the session notes from that day. He could not find any notes in the file from Marlowe, other than sessions with Dr. Ripley. Philip had spoken with Dr. Ripley many times over the past two years regarding Elizabeth. The sessions with Elizabeth Dr. Ripley described were quite different from the experience he was having with the same patient.

Next, he called California Child and Family Services to speak with Elizabeth's former case worker. They had spoken only once before. They planned to meet the next afternoon to review Elizabeth's case file.

Philip made one more call before his next patient was due. He called the California Mental Health Services Oversight and Accountability Commission. He made an appointment to meet with the chair of the Services Committee later in the week.

AS LIZ CLIMBED THE STEPS of her apartment complex, she could hear the lively voices of the tenants who were surrounding the lit grill in the courtyard. She quickly changed out of her work shirt into a teal blouse she felt brought her everyday jeans and sneakers up a notch in style. Looking at her simple collection of slacks and blouses that hung in the closet, she smiled. She did not own a single dress in this realm. She gathered up the chicken breast, cookies, roll and a diet soda into a bag. As she reached for the front door handle, there was a knock. She looked through the peephole. It was Noah. She opened the door.

"Hello," she said.

"Hi, I thought we could go down together," he said.

"Sure," she said.

She walked out to the terrace walkway and locked the door to her apartment behind her. They walked down the steps and turned in towards the courtyard. Noah introduced her to some other tenants. Evelyn was especially happy to see her.

"Would you like one?" Noah asked as he opened his small cooler of beer.

"No, thank you. I'm only twenty," she answered.

"Oh Sweetie, we won't tell anyone," Evelyn said.

"I am glad for the offer, but I'd rather not," Liz said.

"You are a rule follower," Noah stated. "I respect that." He closed his cooler.

Liz smiled. *A rule follower indeed.* She was careful to obey every rule and law in this world. The time she had spent institutionalized at Marlowe made her wary of any other form of incarceration. She never wanted to be a prisoner again.

"Your accent is so unique," Evelyn said. "Has anyone told you that?" She didn't wait for an answer. "Where are you from? British?"

"I am from California. Born in Sacramento." That was true. She had a birth certificate in her personal safe under her bed that said so. It was tangible evidence of her birth in this realm. "My mother was English." People were generally happy with that answer. She couldn't tell a stranger the real reason she sounded like the love child of a hobbit and a valley girl.

She had a pleasant evening. Noah grilled the chicken for her. Evelyn played some music through speakers in the window of her manager's quarters. People ate and drank while they sat on the garden benches that were symmetrically placed within the courtyard. Noah was chatty. Liz learned he had recently graduated with an Associate's Degree in Sociology from Yuba College. Noah was off to continue his education at Sac State this fall. He worked part-time at a bike shop in Yuba City to pay the rent.

Sociology? Wouldn't he get a kick out of my back story, Liz thought.

Liz monitored the time. At eight o'clock, she stood up and told the group that it was time for her to get ready for bed.

"So early?" Evelyn asked.

"Yes, I have early morning plans tomorrow," Liz answered. "I had a lovely time. Thank you."

"I hope we see you again next Tuesday," Evelyn said.

"Sure," Liz said.

"I'll walk you up," Noah said.

"That's unnecessary." Liz did not want to encourage him.

"I'm going up anyway," he said.

They walked up the steps quietly. At the top of the steps, Liz turned and wished him a good night.

"Wait," he said. "Would you like to go out sometime?"

"I'm sorry, Noah, but I'm involved with someone else."

"Oh," he was obviously taken aback. "Oh…I…uh…I never saw you with anyone."

"Leonardo. He's not from around here," she answered.

"Oh," he looked away, then he smiled. "Lucky guy. Forget I asked. Please forget I asked. I'm so embarrassed."

"Don't be," she said. "I had a really nice time tonight."

"Then I'm glad you came. Good night."

"Good night."

She wanted to run to her apartment, but she kept her cadence normal. She unlocked the door and nodded to Noah, who was still at the top of the stairs. He waited until she was inside before he turned to go to his own apartment.

Liz quickly changed into her pajamas. She looked down and noted that the pajamas were cotton, not satin. *For now!* Smiling, she went to the medicine cabinet and took out two antihistamine capsules. Then she poured a glass of water and washed the pills down. She double checked the locks on her front door. Then the locks on her window which faced the courtyard and pulled the blinds down. After she set the music player in her bedroom to the tranquil sounds of trickling waterfalls, she laid down on her bed. Moments after she closed her eyes, the transformation was complete.

2

HADLEIGH, SUFFOLK, ENGLAND - 1555

Elizabeth woke in the early morning before the sun rose. She pulled back her bedding and smiled as she touched the satin nightdress and remembered the cotton pajamas of the other world. She delighted in the scent of fresh lavender which was sewn into her feather mattress. She pushed back the canopy of her bed and tied it back loosely.

It was very dark in her bedchamber. She had one window which was covered by drapes each evening. Shivering as her feet touched the cold stone floor, she opened the door of her bedchamber to steal a flame from the hallway torch. Then used it to light a few candles around her room. She went to her wardrobe and selected a lovely, yet durable, riding gown, along with some leather riding boots. Her wardrobe here was the opposite of her closet in the future, in that it *only* contained dresses and their accoutrements. She had petticoats, corsets, and cotehardies.

It was cumbersome to dress in this world. If she did

not wake up so early, she could employ the help of her handmaiden, Joan. Instead, Elizabeth had studied the time zone differences between Hadleigh and Marysville to plan her sleep schedule in the other world to optimize the time she spent awake in this world. Years ago, she had discovered a direct correlation between the time she went to sleep in Marysville and the time she woke in Hadleigh. It would be another hour before Joan would be available. If she took the promotion that Daphne offered, she would wake a little later in this world. For now, she dressed herself and brushed her long auburn hair. She secured her hair in a simple bun with a jeweled pin. Joan could help her later, if she dressed again for afternoon tea.

The sun started to glow on the horizon as Elizabeth snuffed the candles in her room and made her way to the great hall for breakfast. Her father was also an early riser. Sheep farmers leased most of the land he managed. He went out each morning to connect with the farmers and ensure all was in order. Elizabeth accompanied her father on his routes a few times. She always came prepared to offer research or advice to help the community thrive. While her modern insight was unknown to her father, she found they did not need it in this area. Her father and his farmers showed tremendous expertise regarding the care of the animals and efficiency in shearing, packaging and transporting the wool. She and her father usually took a small breakfast together before he started his route. This morning, he was waiting for her at the bottom of the staircase.

"Good morrow, my beauteous daughter."

His smile beamed as she took his hand to enter the

hall together. The house staff had set the table with bread and a bowl of fruit the night before. Large clay domes covered the food to deter rodents from nibbling in the night. Since she and her father were such early risers, the house staff rarely assembled for their duties in time to serve a proper breakfast meal. She and her father preferred having the time to themselves. After she washed her hands in a nearby basin, she took an apple from the fruit bowl and tore off a crust of bread. She sat at the table next to her father. She thought, if she took the promotion in the other realm, she would have to give up these mornings alone with her father. He poured them both glasses of mint infused spring water.

"I see thou art fitted for a ride this morning," her father observed her attire.

"Yea, Father. There is a stream at the south border I would like to paint today," she lied a little.

"Thou art like thy mother in so many ways. She, too, was transfixed by the south border." He bit into an apple while he looked at his daughter adoringly. "Thy resemblance to her is quite strong of late. Thou hast my eyes, but thou carry her features in thy face and hair."

"Father, art thou feeling well? It seems thou art particularly nostalgic this morning." She walked around the table to place her arm on his shoulder.

"This day is the anniversary of my marriage to thy mother."

"I am sorry. It did not occur to me, Father." she looked guiltily at her lap. She had never told him what she knew of her mother in the other realm.

"Do not vex thyself, child. 'Twould be unusual for thou to recall a date which hath never been celebrated in thy lifetime." He took a long drink of water from his chalice. "I shall be in the village for a good portion of the day, but I shall be home in time for supper. Whilst thou bring thy creation for viewing tonight?"

"Certainly, Father," she replied.

Elizabeth finished her apple and wrapped the chunk of bread in a cloth to bring with her. She grabbed a few more apples and took them to the small room her father had made available to her on the first floor to use for her varied interests. The room had a small shelf of handwritten books from this era. She possessed stacks of parchment, crude paper, and vellum for her personal use. Paper was becoming more accessible each year, but her collection was still meager. She made the most of her paltry stash by documenting only the highlights of her time on the other side. On this morning, she wrote a bit about the barbecue she had attended at the apartment complex the night before. Afterwards, she gathered her paints, brushes, and a small canvas and placed them into a saddlebag. She brought her bag to the bench in the foyer and waited for Joan.

Joan arrived dutifully with the full rising of the morning sun. Her father employed Joan as her handmaiden, but Elizabeth rarely sought her services unless absolutely necessary. Joan held more value in another capacity, as her best friend. Elizabeth confided in her without reservation.

"Good morrow, Lady Elizabeth," Joan smiled at her friend.

"Good morrow to thee," Elizabeth hopped off the bench to greet her friend.

Each morning, their greetings held much exuberance.

Joan looked forward to hearing the daily recap, which always waited until their posse had assembled in secret. She knew while she slept each night, Elizabeth was experiencing an extra daytime in the other realm.

Elizabeth, as the daughter of a nobleman, could not go out in public without a chaperone. Joan was always her companion. Bennet joined the two ladies on most excursions as well. He worked in the stables on the property. He was also trusted to be aware of Elizabeth's double life. Bennet and Joan had fallen in love with each other over the past few years. Elizabeth approved of the match greatly. She trusted Bennet and Joan above all others. They loved her and would protect her with their lives if needed. They kept many secrets for Elizabeth, including her rendezvous with Leonardo near the south border.

"Where might we go today, my lady?" Joan asked, looking at the saddlebag.

"We shall fetch Bennet and ride to the stream at the south border," Elizabeth winked at her friend. "I have *my* painting utensils."

"'Tis going to be a lovely day for painting, my lady," Joan took the saddlebag from Elizabeth's hands and headed towards the door before Elizabeth had the chance to complain that she could carry her own bag.

It was a quick walk to the stables. Three horses stood saddled and ready to go. Bennet greeted the women with a bow.

"Good morrow, Bennet," Elizabeth snatched her saddle bag from Joan and secured it to her mare, Cheerio. The others found the name of her horse strange, but Elizabeth had been young when she acquired the mare. She named her after the cereal her foster parents fed her continuously in the other world. It was one of the few things she could bring herself to eat there. All other cereals had been too sweet and artificial tasting, given her palate from this world.

"Good morrow, my lady," Bennet smiled. He followed Elizabeth and double-checked her procedures with the horse, which irritated her greatly. "Might I venture a guess for our course today?" He smirked. "The stream at the south border?"

Elizabeth smiled back at him and mounted Cheerio. Bennet turned to Joan so he could capture her hand and bring it quickly to his lips for a kiss. Joan rewarded him with a huge smile. They each mounted their horses, and the trio rode to the stream. It was a brief ride. Bennet dismounted first and helped each woman to the ground. He then unpacked the items he had brought along. He laid a large blanket on the ground. Elizabeth contributed the apples and bread from her pack. She handed the painting supplies over to Bennet.

"I promised Father I would bring back a masterpiece," she winked at him. Bennet eagerly accepted the task. A rock was used to prop up the small canvas. He put some of the water from the stream into a cup and gathered some other elements of nature to assist his rudimentary easel set up. Leaves to be used to squeeze the brush dry between color changes. A smooth piece of tree bark to use as a palette. He was soon happily engaged with his art as Joan rested on the blanket nearby, watching.

Elizabeth sat near the bank of the stream, watching the direction Leonardo would come from. It wasn't long before she could make out the top of his head coming toward her over a hill. He waved, and she waved back. She watched each stride eagerly. She thought most girls from the other realm would not give Leonardo a second glance. His light brown hair was thin and straight. He kept it tied back neatly. His frame was thin, and his height was average. His skin was bronze from both his Spanish lineage and the time he spent outdoors over the summer. They could only meet a few days each week. The absence between each meeting, of course, felt longer for her than it did for him.

He came to the place in the stream where he could cross. There were several boulders naturally placed, which provided a bridge for the physically adept. Leonardo was well practiced on this particular path. He easily strode across each rock. As he neared, she stood. Her heartbeat faster with the love and excitement she felt for him. He held her and kissed her, not lustfully, but with the tenderness of love.

"Hello," she whispered.

"Hello," he murmured back.

"Shall we get married today?" she asked coyly.

"In my loveliest dreams, we have already been man and wife for ages," he responded.

"I am becoming an old maid," she teased. "I think my father will notice soon."

"Shall we approach him today? Yea, even without a title, he might respect my work. Dost thou agree?" He asked.

"My darling, I am so happy to hear these words. This is not the time to approach him. Thoughts of my mother sadden him this day. Today would have been their wedding anniversary. Perhaps we shall have a meal with him next week?"

"So be it. In the meantime, let us continue our work to free thee from the disembodied curse from which thou suffer. I have found some writings in my father's library that may help. Pray thee, tell about thy latest experiences in the other world." He led her to the blanket, and they sat down next to Joan.

Elizabeth told them of her Tuesday in California. She told them of the offer of promotion at her job, her appointment with Dr. Sawyer, and the barbecue with her neighbors in the apartment complex. She felt it best not to mention the interest Noah had shown in her romantically. As usual, they all listened intently. Their mouths hanging open at times. Every breath of her recounting still seemed so incredible to them. No matter how many times Elizabeth regaled them with her experiences, they just couldn't imagine a *woman* living on her own so self-sufficiently! *Just wait until Queen Elizabeth begins her reign*, she thought. Past conversations about electricity, automobiles, and telephones had been equally enthralling.

"Quite incredible," Leonardo uttered after she had finished. "I have continued to pore over my father's books and journals. I have found a spell that seems similar to thy predicament, but 'tis not quite right. 'Tis a spell to separate the good and the evil from a person into two different forms. It creates a demon and an angel. I think it could be related to what happened to thee, but thou hast two of the same versions of thyself. One 'tis hither and one thither. Both versions art extraordinarily good." He reached over to tuck a stray hair behind her ear and stroke her cheek.

"This place certainly seems more like heaven and the other like hell. But I agree, I am the same person in both places," she conceded.

She was hopeful they were close to solving the mystery of her ailment. Leonardo's father, Matias Navarro, was a renowned sorcerer of sorts in the area. Elizabeth thought it would be another point of contention when they sought her father's approval of their marriage. Matias was the reason that Leonardo and Elizabeth met. Matias' reputation as a wizard was locally renowned. She had sought him out two years prior. She had crossed the south border seeking audience with Matias, but had met Leonardo instead. He had been performing an experiment with the wind to power a mechanical wheat grinder. She admired his innovation. That day she had learned Matias had left on a quest six months before.

The sparks of attraction came fast and easy for Elizabeth and Leonardo. She had felt an immediate connection with him. She trusted him and opened up to him about her troubles. He vowed to help her. She had taken care to help him with her modern knowledge. They created some inventions that would be useful for the time, but would not disrupt the history of industrialization. She brought him knowledge of advanced farming techniques, such as the importance of soil composition and fertilization. He used the knowledge to become a paid consultant of sorts to other farming communities in the countryside. Most of the noblemen in England sought his guidance for reaping the best crops they could for their lands. His work in this capacity, while well compensated, required a great deal of travel. This was the reason he and Elizabeth could not meet as often as they would like. In his free time, Leonardo read through the documents and journals that his father had left in his study. His father had, unfortunately, taken the best of his spells with him on his quest.

Even if they were to have the luck of finding the right spell, there were doubts they could administer a spell without Matias. Leonardo had shown no signs of inheriting his father's gift. There had been little word from him since he left. There was no way to contact him, as his communications showed he was moving from city to city and country to country quickly. It forced them to wait for his return and hope it would be soon.

"I have an idea," Joan said. "Let us go over all the specifics we know about thy condition. Maybe a retelling will sprout new ideas and topics for Leonardo to research."

"Alright," Elizabeth took a deep breath. "Twenty years ago, in 1535, I was born here in Hadleigh, Suffolk and simultaneously, in a place called Sacramento, California in the year 1995. Accounts from my governess in this era suggest that my father, along with my mother's birthing ladies, discovered me abandoned by my mother moments after birth in her bedchamber. He cleaned me up and placed me under the care of the ladies while he searched for my mother. In this time, her whereabouts art still unknown.

In the 1995 timeline, doctors discovered my mother in labor outside a bakery in Sacramento. An ambulance was called to the bakery." She paused. "An ambulance is emergency transport for medical professionals." She looked to each member of her group to confirm they were following her recounting. "They took her to Mercy General Hospital. In the other world, I have a *birth* certificate from the hospital. This is a legal document that lists my mother as Katharine Percy and my father as Richard Percy. My mother must've been conscious to provide that information. She died a few hours later from complications of the birth. I have a *death* certificate providing that information as well. I have lived two lifetimes each day since. My father has raised me here in Hadleigh, and I was in various foster homes as a child in Sacramento. A foster family is one which is compensated to care for orphan children or those deemed endangered by their natural parents. I didn't stay in one foster home too long. As I gained trust in the people I lived with, I would try to confide about my dual lives to an adult or another child. Each time, the same result. They thought I was mad. Eventually, Child Protective Services committed me to Marlowe Psychiatric Hospital, a place where they keep people with abnormal mental conditions. The doctor there diagnosed me with a disease called schizophrenia. This, of course, is not the case. Instead, by some supernatural occurrence, each night that I go to bed in California, I instantly awake in this timeline."

"I never confided in my father," she continued. "He was not available for much of my childhood. I know 'twas painful for him to be around me as he missed my mother a great deal. He left from time to time to search for her. When I was old enough to understand that she was dead in the future timeline, I did not know if that meant she had vanished from this timeline as well.

Given that my mother is nowhere to be found in this timeline, we assume, like her, if I die in one timeline, then I will die in the other as well.

When I turned eighteen in the year 2013, the state released me from Marlowe Psychiatric Hospital. When a person reaches the age of eighteen in the future, they are considered an adult and can live on their own. I moved to a nearby town called Marysville. My social worker worked with my former psychiatrist for the state of California to provide out-patient mental care until my twenty-first birthday. I found employment and my out-patient care was transferred to a local psychiatrist, Dr. Philip Sawyer. I have met with him every Tuesday since. I hope to convince him I have given up my delusions and built a simple life in the future timeline. I will be free of his care on my twenty-first birthday. 'Twere the terms of the state court mandated upon my release from Marlowe."

She paused to look at her friends. They were all listening as intently as they had before. Elizabeth pulled out some papers she had written on. She showed them to her friends.

"Here is a chart I made of the time zone differences between what will be known as Marysville, California in the future and here, Hadleigh, Suffolk. Doth thou see, the timing is seamless when I go to sleep in California around 8 o'clock in the evening and awake here at 5 o'clock in the morning? But 'tis not reliable because there is extra time. My soul truly exists in two bodies simultaneously. When I wake in Marysville, 'tis between 6 and 7 o'clock the next morning there, and still mid-afternoon here in Hadleigh. The transition is seamless. I hop from this form to the other in a moment. As my friends, thou hast all witnessed that I do not miss a beat during transition. My life here continues on throughout the night as we all experience here in Hadleigh. At the same time, I wake in the future world and go about my day. When I wake here, my mind instantly hath the knowledge of the events of the previous day here in Hadleigh. From this information, we know that I have one soul sharing two bodies with over 400 years separating them." Elizabeth paused and looked around the group again. Each person was holding their most intense, thoughtful pose. Leonardo, Joan and Bennet, each would love to provide a theory, or even better, a solution to help their friend.

"And last, we know I am the most fortunate person in the entire world to have friends like you," she smiled fondly at them all.

Leonardo had been taking notes and reviewing past documents the entire time Elizabeth had been speaking. He reached over to take the chart with the time zones she had shown the group. Time zones were a very foreign concept for this era. Mechanical clocks were not yet commonplace, and it would be hundreds of years before the Prime Meridian would be implemented.

"Absolutely brilliant. May I keep this?" he asked.

"Aye, of course," Elizabeth responded.

He tucked the chart inside the other papers he had brought inside a journal. He would have plenty of time to review the chart and his notes before their next rendezvous.

They watched as Bennet created a beautiful painting of the stream and surrounding hills. He took frequent breaks to smile at Joan. When he finished the painting, he set it to dry. Leonardo supplied Bennet with additional paper and charcoal. Bennet drew an incredibly lifelike portrait of Joan. The morning continued happily as the two couples chatted together and shared the bits of food they had brought with them. She was sad to break up the group, but as mistress of her father's estate, she had inherited many responsibilities that needed attending to. The group stood and packed away their belongings. Bennet and Joan led the horses to the stream for a drink so that Elizabeth could have a few moments of privacy with Leonardo.

"Three days. 'Tis too long to see thee again," he whispered.

"'Tis twice as long for me," she said.

"I know. We shall find a solution. I promise," he said.

"If anyone will find one, 'tis thou," she smiled. "I don't have to work tomorrow, in Marysville, that is. I will go to the library. There are several books I requested to be put on hold that should be ready for me."

"'Tis truly remarkable! Oh, how I would love if I could travel with thee to the year 2015. To have access to thy Internet, libraries, and universities would be such a great treat!" He was lost in thought for a moment.

"Thou will have to believe me that 'tis so much better here. There is so much that is unspoiled here. Here, where so much is yet to be discovered. Here with thee, my friends and my father." She placed her hand on his chest and felt his heartbeat. "I love thee."

"I love thee," he said back to her. They enjoyed another parting kiss and went their separate ways.

Elizabeth returned to her home. The household staff

was waiting to meet with her. She was very efficient at running the household. Soon, the menu was planned for the entire week. She discussed the laundry requirements for the guest rooms that hadn't been aired out in some time. It was near time to change seasonal décor, so she directed which cases should be brought down from the attic rooms. The day went quickly and without incident. At mid-afternoon, her transition to 2015 occurred without notice to anyone around her.

3

WEDNESDAY, AUGUST 5, 2015 MARYSVILLE, CA

Again, Liz awoke to the sounds of a modern era. She could hear the refrigerator compressor humming from the nearby kitchen as it was located a mere five feet from her bed. Even with the window closed, she could hear someone's futile attempt to start a car engine that just wouldn't turn over. She also heard something unexpected. Someone was knocking at her door!

She walked to the front door of her apartment and looked through the peephole. It was Dr. Sawyer. She looked down at her pajamas. She shrugged her shoulders as she deemed them to be decent enough and opened the door.

"Dr. Sawyer, I wasn't expecting you," she said.

"Quite right. This is an unscheduled visit to observe your living conditions," he stated. She noticed his hands were full, carrying a drink holder with two coffees and a bag, presumably of donuts or pastries, judging by the logo on the bag.

"Won't you come in?" She stepped aside to allow him passage.

"Thank you," he said. He walked in and set the items down on her desk/table.

This was the first time Dr. Sawyer had performed an inspection of her apartment. It made her think of the times her social worker had inspected the homes of her foster parents when she was young. The social worker she had now was also mandated to conduct four inspections per year, but it seemed less invasive an activity than it had been when she was a child.

"Might I have just a moment to change into something more presentable?" she asked.

"Of course," he said. He picked up one coffee and made himself comfortable on her small sofa.

Liz shut the door to her bedroom. This visit excited her. She knew it was a sign that her therapy was going well enough that he wanted to gather further evidence to petition for a reduction of her mandatory therapy. She dressed quickly.

She stepped out of her room with a big smile that fell flat when she saw her doctor reading a paper she had left on her desk. It was a copy of her time zone analysis between Hadleigh and Marysville. There were other pieces of documentation on the desk that she hadn't thought of. She had notes and photocopies from her trips to the library.

"Hadleigh is the place from your delusions, isn't it?" he asked.

Liz felt the color drain from her face, but she was quick.

"Yes, it is. I have been researching it recently. It is a

real place. Though it is quite different from the delusional portrayal I gave in my youth."

"Why haven't you brought up this research in our sessions?" he asked.

"I didn't know what you would think," she replied.

"I think it is normal and healthy for you to be curious. I am pleased to hear you found it different from the imaginary world you had created. Were you seeking this information for validation?" he asked.

"No, of course not. Like you said, I was curious." She was still on edge, wondering how his discovery of her research would affect his decisions about the frequency or the need to continue out-patient therapy.

He took a drink of coffee while he regarded her, then turned back to the time zone chart. He picked up the second coffee and handed it to her.

"It is black. I brought cream and sweeteners if you like." He guided her over to the sofa and set the coffee cup on the table in front of her. "Did you have plans today?"

"Nothing firm. I have some errands and a trip to the library," she responded. She felt frozen in place as he walked around the counter to her kitchenette.

"We can do those things together today. I will just make observations." He took another drink of coffee. "May I?" he asked as he pointed at her cabinets. She nodded, and he opened one near her stove. Locating a plate, he took it down. He opened the bag and placed croissants and fruit pastries on the plate. He then placed the plate in front of her as well. Liz exhaled slowly. She picked up her coffee and took a tiny sip. It was good. Dark and full-bodied. She knew she shouldn't drink too much. It had been years since she had ingested caffeine in any significant amount. She preferred at least ten hours of sleep per night, and caffeine was counter-intuitive to that goal. She was nervous enough about Dr. Sawyer's inspection that she did not want the coffee to give her additional jitters. He peeked through her remaining cabinets and looked inside the refrigerator and freezer.

"I'm just going to look at the rest of your apartment," he said.

He waited for her nod of affirmation before he slipped into the bedroom and bathroom area. He was only gone a few minutes. Liz heard the sound of her closet door opening, then her shower curtain, and finally her medicine cabinet. She forced herself to breathe slow and normal during the process. She knew he would not find any illegal materials or substances in her apartment, but she was in a naturally nervous state to have someone who studies her mind looking through her personal effects. What if he thought she had too many red shirts and applied color psychology logic to determine she had lustful thoughts or faced negative issues that she never relayed to him? What if he analyzed the way she stored her toiletries or arranged her furniture? Having a psychiatrist perform a home inspection was quite a different experience than having a social worker perform the same duty. He returned and gave her a reassuring smile. He sat next to her on the small sofa.

"There are no recordings today. When I return to my office, I will make notes. I want you to know that our conversations today are off the record. I will not report anything we talk about unless you want me to. You probably recognize this as an inspection to reduce your mandatory therapy, but I would rather you see it as an opportunity to confide in me." He reached down and took a croissant.

"Dr. Sawyer, I already tell you everything." She was nervous.

"Liz, I have read all the files from your time at Marlowe Psychiatric Hospital. You gave such elaborate descriptions of the double life you were living. You felt the dual existence your whole life. Then, suddenly, it stopped? It is as if the other life disappeared on a timer."

It was the first time Dr. Sawyer had ever expressed any skepticism about her recovery. Liz remained quiet. She carefully placed the cup of coffee back on the table.

"Liz, it isn't recommended practice for someone in my profession to confront a patient with a delusional disorder. But that is exactly what I am going to do now. I don't believe in magic and you have had no sort of physical injury or mental distress to switch off the delusions. A sudden recovery, such that you portray, has never happened with a patient before."

Liz felt panic rising in every cell in her body. *What was happening? Why now? Dr. Sawyer has been a passive listener in her sessions for two years! Why is he doing this?* She remained silent.

Philip could sense her growing panic. He knew he needed to jolt her, but didn't want to take it too far. He changed to a softer tone.

"Liz, I want you to relax. I know that is easier said than done. I am not a threat to you. You are never going back to Marlowe Psychiatric Hospital as long as I am your doctor. I promise you that."

Liz cocked her head slightly. He had her full attention.

"You were going to be released on your eighteenth birthday regardless of prognosis. You were only there because you were a minor and a ward of the state. Delusional disorders are generally treated on an outpatient basis. I'm still not even sure how they pulled off a schizophrenic diagnosis, to be honest with you." He leaned back and observed her reaction. She remained silent.

"I mentioned before, we are off the record. If you are still experiencing the double life here and in Hadleigh, I would like for you to feel comfortable enough to confide in me. We could use our sessions to make the co-existence easier for you. You could talk to me instead of keeping it all bottled up inside. That is the best therapy available for people with delusions. I could be your confidant, and be assured, confidentiality is of utmost importance in my profession. Now, I have just seen your stockpile of antihistamines, melatonin, and GABA. They have been present on your toxicology screens regularly. Are you using these products to induce sleep?"

"Off the record?" she finally spoke.

"Yes," he was hopeful.

"This is a freebie? I can tell you anything at all and it will not go into my record, nor will it change my current treatment conditions?"

"Correct." He tried to keep his tone even and not appear overexcited.

"I do not suffer delusions," she said.

He deflated. He was sure that she still perceived a double life, yet was cleverly masking it from the public.

"Because it is real," she continued. "And I do believe

in magic. You said you don't believe in magic. I do."

He was hopeful again.

"I can prove it," she said.

"Show me," he said.

Liz walked over to pick up her laptop and brought it back to the sofa. She opened a browser and first searched for the Duke of Redam in 1532. A painting of her father showed up in the image results. A Wikipedia entry was the first in the web search results. She clicked on it and passed the laptop to Philip.

"This is my father, His Grace, Richard Percy," she stated.

Philip looked at the web article. The image in the corner was small. He looked up at her. She was serious. He read the text within the entry. It was a small paragraph. Not much was known about this Duke. His title was short-lived. He died in 1562 with no male heir to carry on the crest. Philip knew these sorts of internet entries could be forged or impossible to validate. He did not contradict her. She might have made the entry herself and blocked it out to support her fantasy. He wanted her to continue to confide in him.

Liz went to her bedroom and pulled a small suitcase style safe from under her bed. She opened it and pulled out a document and brought it to him. It was her birth certificate, with the official seal, listing Katharine and Richard Percy as her biological parents. He looked up from the document to see her watching him in earnest.

"Thank you for sharing this with me. Could we talk about how you have been living with this knowledge for the past two years?"

Liz showed him the time zone chart again. She

explained the transformation and how the time gaps caught up with her a day later. She told him of her friends and confidants who seem to exist simultaneously in the past. Of Leonardo and his father, Matias, who was a renowned wizard of that time. It was their belief that Matias could be capable of a spell to unite the two souls that span separate timelines into one.

"Which timeline do you hope to become whole in?" Philip asked.

"I hope to become whole in the 1550's. That is where my father is, and Leonardo. I want to marry Leonardo. There is nothing for me here in 2015." She looked around the tiny apartment.

He knew she would choose the alternate life. It was common for patients with delusional disorders to prefer their fantasies over real life. In the illusion she has created, she has wealth, family, friends and a love interest. Her real life is isolating, with a meager income and no family. She might never give up the alternate reality she has created in her mind, but he might be able to get her to make slight changes in real life that would lead to some measure of happiness.

"What did you say your plans were before I showed up today?" he asked.

"I was going to the library to do more research," she said. "We are trying to find reference to Matias. If we can find him, we can ask him to come home and help. Leonardo does not know where he goes when he takes off. He leaves for years at a time and comes back to check on his household briefly before he is off again. The local library here in Marysville has very limited resources, but I can request books from other libraries I find in the online catalog. It doesn't open until noon today."

"Why don't I take you to the campus library at Cal State? It is open to the public and I still hold an Alumni Borrower's card. Anything you check out, you can return to me at our next session."

"'Twould be amazing!" Liz was very excited, and it showed. Her entire time in this realm had been miserable and lonely. It was an enormous relief to have someone in this time to talk to about the condition of her split soul.

"It will take us about an hour to drive there. I realize I came very early this morning. I didn't want to risk missing you. Would you like to have a shower? I can wait outside," he offered.

"A shower would be lovely. Are you sure you don't mind?" she asked.

"Not at all. It is a beautiful morning, and I would like to take a better look at your courtyard," he said.

He gathered up his coffee and croissant and stepped outside. He heard the tumble of the lock on the door behind him. It really was a perfect California morning outside. The sun was shining into the open courtyard. The property manager maintained it well. It added more elegance to such a plain building structure with the smallest living quarters he had ever seen. As he sipped his coffee, he noticed a young man leaving his apartment with a lightweight road bike slung over a shoulder. The young man was wearing a full cycling kit. He looked over and Philip gave him a nod. The young man stared at him hard for a full ten seconds before he remembered his manners and gave a wave back. The man surprised Philip when he came right over.

"Are you Liz's…um…" he started.

"Uncle," Philip answered and watched as the young man relaxed. "She's inside getting ready. Are you a friend?"

"As much as she will let me. I'm Noah," he said and reached out a hand. Philip shook hands with the young man and gave him a mental once over. Noah was a very attractive kid with a well-developed physique. Likely from cycling.

"That's a nice ride you have there," Philip genuinely admired the model of bike that Noah had. He had been an avid cyclist himself in his youth. Not that Philip was very old himself. He just had a lot more responsibility running his own practice than he did ten years ago.

"Thanks," Noah replied. "It gets me around." Noah clearly wanted to ask him something but was having trouble getting up the nerve.

"What's your story?" Philip asked.

"Not much yet," Noah responded. "I finished my second year at Yuba."

"Major?"

"Sociology."

Philip raised an eyebrow. Interesting.

"Any plans after you get your Associate's?" Philip asked.

"I am transferring to Cal State in Sacramento," he replied.

"Oh yeah? We are visiting the campus today," Philip volunteered.

"Really? Is Liz thinking of attending?" Noah asked.

"I'll do my best, but it's not likely."

"Yeah," Noah looked at the ground.

"Cal State is close, but it's still quite the daily commute. You planning on sticking around this complex?" Philip countered.

"If I had a good reason," Noah answered honestly.

Philip smiled at the younger man. Noah could be additional leverage for Liz to choose this world if she gave him a chance. A sociology major would likely be patient and understanding of her recovery.

Liz opened the door to come out. She caught sight of Noah in his tight-fitting cycling gear and immediately blushed and cast her eyes downward. This was her usual response to his riding kit, and he found it charming.

"Good morning, Liz," Noah greeted her with a smile. "Just chatting with your uncle. You two have a great day." He made his way down to the courtyard. Philip and Liz waited until the clicking of his cycling shoes subsided on the concrete steps before they started walking down to the parking lot.

"Uncle?" she asked.

"Of course. It isn't my place to reveal the true nature of our relationship."

He led her to his car. It was a nice sedan. It wasn't a luxury model, but it was a higher end car than she had ever sat in. After they were buckled in, he set the navigation for the CSUS Library. She watched the route guidance recommendations and was fascinated once again by modern day technology. As they pulled out of the parking lot, she was also struck by how smooth a ride it was. Her own car was not nearly as comfortable.

"Tell me about the barbecue you attended here last night. Did you make any new friends?" he asked.

"The barbecue was lovely. My neighbors were very

welcoming. Noah is the one who invited me. Well, he made a pass at me. I told him I was in a relationship. He was understandably skeptical. It isn't as if my neighbors will ever see Leonardo come and pick me up for a date."

"I'm glad to hear you are socializing. There is no reason your life here should be so lonely." he glanced over at her. She was looking at the road ahead, but he could tell that she was processing the information.

"You're right," she whispered. "It doesn't hurt to make new friends. I guess I never wanted to get too close to anyone in this realm because I didn't want anyone to miss me when I'm gone."

"Gone? You mean if there is magic to reunite the two souls?" he asked cautiously.

"I know what you are getting at. Suicide. I won't lie. I have considered it. Given that my mother and I came here together and the fact that she was nowhere to be found in Hadleigh in 1535 after her recorded death here in Sacramento in 1995, I am led to believe that if a body dies in one realm, it will vanish in the other." She spoke as a matter of fact.

Philip nodded his head. Her logic was encouraging and led naturally to self-preservation. Perhaps he could convince her to apply her intelligence in this 'realm'.

"Tell me about your job. What made you choose the job as a retail cashier?" he asked.

"When I left Marlowe, I didn't have any previous working experience or college education. They were hiring, and the position was entry level. I have been fortunate to keep a regular daytime schedule. Yesterday, my boss offered a management level position, but with evening hours. I will owe her an answer on Friday."

"Why wouldn't you take the position? I assume it offers a higher wage?"

"Yes, it does. I'm considering it. I checked the time zone table. Our store closes at 10pm each evening. I would have to move my sleeping schedule here back a bit, which might cause me to wake a bit later in the other realm. My father is also an early riser and, by waking later, I would miss our private breakfasts together. He manages our land that is leased to sheep farmers. He likes to get out early to make the rounds and stay in touch with the farmers. Perhaps my other body will continue to wake at five o'clock in the morning. I will absorb the memories of my breakfast with my father during the overlap of the souls when I sleep here. I have, in the past, experienced a queer correlation to my sleeping and waking patterns between the realms. There are many benefits of having mornings and early afternoons free in this realm. It would give me more opportunities during the daytime to visit the library during business hours and research the magic I need in 1555 to make me whole. The salary increase would also be appreciated."

"I see," he said. He was kicking himself for not intervening sooner. He recognized her delusion was deeply entrenched in every aspect of her life. They had a lot of work ahead of them.

For the rest of the drive, she told him more about Bennet and Joan. About how she confided in them and how they kept her secrets and helped her to meet with Leonardo. She recounted the many picnics and paintings that had happened by the stream in the past two years. He smiled when she described her horse, Cheerio. She discussed how she and Leonardo planned to approach her father for permission to marry.

She stopped speaking as they drove onto the campus of California State University in Sacramento. There were so many people her age walking to class, chatting with each other, holding hands, and milling about. Philip drove to a parking structure near the library.

As they walked from the parking structure to the library, the size of the campus overwhelmed Liz and she was even more impressed when she saw the size of the library itself. When they walked inside, she studied the inventory listed next to each level. There were five floors plus a lower level. Philip knew the library well from his time as a student. He directed her to the elevators.

"We will start at the south end of the second floor first and migrate up to the north end of the third floor. I believe that is where you will find historical accounts of magic from that era. We can check the kiosks, to be sure." He pushed the button for the second floor once they were inside the elevator.

When they exited, she stood in awe. Several people walked by her and gave her a quizzical look. Philip was pleased that she was so taken by the extensive collection held by the CSUS library.

"My eyes hath never seen such a glorious repository," Liz whispered.

"Excuse me?" asked Dr. Sawyer.

He led her to a kiosk and taught her how to search by subject. After giving her a brief lay of the land, he showed her the table where he would sit and wait for her.

"Take your time. I have cleared my schedule for most of the day." He then sat at the nearby table and took out his notebook. He made notes of the conversations of the day. Although he had agreed to keep it all off the record, he wanted to have private notes for himself that he could review later. He would not include these in her formal file without her express permission. They could discuss the benefits of keeping her experience on file when they had lunch later.

The kiosk system was easy and intuitive to use. She established a triangular path between the kiosk, the racks and the table where Philip sat. The book piles grew in size. Then she would sort them by scanning the contents and make a small pile of 'keepers'. She was dutiful in returning the books that would not be useful. She felt no need to create more work for the library staff, particularly with her 'guest' status. An hour later, she had three books under her arm and was ready to move up to the third floor. After another hour of her scouring the racks, he interrupted her to have lunch. They checked out the books she had selected and went over to the student center on campus to have some quick service deli sandwiches.

It was nearing the end of the summer semester on campus. There weren't too many students around, but more than Philip would have thought. He was pleased. It was good for Liz to be exposed to how some people her age spent their time.

"You know," he began slowly. "If you were to take on the promotion at your job, you could still pursue a higher education."

"I can't say that I have thought about it much before

today. I know I don't make enough money to pay tuition," she looked thoughtful. "But 'twould be nice to have access to all those books. I bet they have a great program here for historical studies."

"Sure, but I don't think you should overlook a future in engineering or computer science."

"Hmmm. Those are areas of study I could only achieve in this realm." She was deep in thought again.

"Also," he continued, "You would likely be eligible for grants and state tuition assistance programs given your low income over the past two years. If there is any remaining tuition for you to pay after applying to those programs, which I doubt, there are always student loans you could easily pay back after you finish your degree and land a better-paying job."

"I wouldn't know where to begin." She was very overwhelmed.

"Why don't we stop in the visitor's center? We can get you some information and we can use your session next Tuesday to complete the forms together."

"Thank you, Dr. Sawyer. I will definitely give it some thought."

"One other thing. I made some notes while we were in the library regarding all that we have discussed today. Unless you give me permission, I will not include these notes in your file. I told you today was a freebie and off the record. I stand by that. But I also wanted you to know that if we include my notes from today, it would change nothing. You are an adult, and you are managing your condition quite well. You do not pose a threat to yourself or others. The information I wrote about today could be beneficial if something were to happen to me or you were transferred to another therapist." He stopped to gauge her reaction.

"Dr. Sawyer, does this mean that you don't believe me?" she asked.

"I believe you believe. And I believe it is good for you to have someone like me to talk about what you believe. Together, we can openly discuss your experiences. We can bounce ideas off each other like we did today. I can do my best to provide guidance where it could benefit your quality of life."

"You can add your notes to my file. I really hope that nothing happens to you. I quite enjoyed the use of your CSUS library pass today," she smiled.

"About that, you could become a student here and get your own card. Or you could purchase a community borrower's card."

Liz smiled and did a happy little drum roll on the lunch table.

They drove back to Liz's apartment, mostly in silence. There was a lot to think about. She was eager to read the books Dr. Sawyer had borrowed for her. Her mind drifted as she thought about college, her job, and her small apartment. The smooth ride of the doctor's sedan made her also think of her pathetic little car. He pulled into a guest parking space at her complex. She gathered her belongings and stepped out of the car. He left the car running and came around the back of the car to meet her.

"Thank you again, Dr. Sawyer. I really appreciate everything you did for me today. It was nice to have an ear to bend, and it was very impressive to visit the Cal State campus."

"Thank you for trusting me, Liz. Today was a

milestone in our relationship between doctor and patient. One I see as a huge success. I look forward to our session on Tuesday to hear your thoughts on some of the lifestyle changes we discussed today." He squeezed her arm and got back into his car.

After watching his car drive away, she skipped up the stairs to her apartment. She unlocked the door and set all her books down on her little table/desk. She looked around her tiny apartment, thinking about CSUS. If she enrolled there, it would be difficult to commute so far away. She would have to move. She was sure that she could talk to Daphne about a transfer to a Sacramento store. Or she could stay in Marysville and enroll in Yuba College. She knew that was where Noah was going in the fall. He could surely give her information about the school. She continued looking around her apartment, thinking of the two years she had spent here living in the dark shadow of her life in Hadleigh.

Her existence in this realm had not been easy. Liz thought of the foster care and subsequent psychiatric care that she had endured. She had made no friends in this realm. She had acquaintances, but no one she trusted, like Joan and Bennet. It had never occurred to her she could rise above the hand she had been dealt in this realm. She had only been doing as much as it took to survive here. An education would surely lead to a better quality of life and access to better library resources. Friends and a social life might make the time on this side more bearable.

She sat down on her sofa and tuned out the sounds of the modern city. She picked up the most promising looking text she had borrowed that day. It did not contain any information about Matias. It spoke of another famed sorcerer of the 1550s. His name was Simon Fulmer. Thanks to the text, she knew exactly where she could find him in 1555. It was the first night she had gone to sleep in this realm with a smile on her face since she could remember. She was full of hope and couldn't wait to tell Leonardo.

4

HADLEIGH, SUFFOLK, ENGLAND - 1555

Elizabeth woke in the dark and gained the memories of the previous evening in this realm. After their dinner, her father had received a summons to London to discuss some new legislation with the crown. Her father was well liked at court and would likely stay a week or two. Elizabeth had heard talk of a young widow in London that her father frequently engaged for tea. She thought he would probably take this opportunity to visit with the widow. He had never discussed the woman with his daughter, and Elizabeth did not wish to pry. Elizabeth knew he would never move forward with another woman, so long as he had the hope Katharine would return. She had not told him that her mother had died in the other realm and had thus ceased to exist here. She had not spoken to him of the other realm since she was a child. He viewed her stories then as fanciful imaginings of a child. She learned about mental illness and how her stories gave the perception of such when she was admitted to Marlowe Psychiatric Hospital in the other realm. She did not want her father to see her that way, so she stopped telling him the stories. Instead, she had kept the other realm private from him until such a time she could prove its existence. Without a body, he would never believe that Katharine was gone. Also, without a body, he would need to petition for divorce if he wanted to make a commitment to the widow he was so fond of. She doubted the devout Catholic Queen Mary would condone a divorce. If he were to try in a few years when Queen Elizabeth came to reign, his chances would improve.

Quickly, she dressed in a cotehardie and a pair of comfortable leather boots. She had stayed awake longer than usual in the other realm. The textbook she had borrowed on Dr. Sawyer's account had been so engrossing. After learning of the wizard, Simon Fulmer, she had trouble falling asleep, given the excitement she felt. As such, she had woken a bit later in this realm. She feared she would be too late to see her father off on his trip. She relaxed when he walked over to meet her at the bottom of the stairs.

"I am glad I did not miss thee," she said as she wrapped her arms around him.

"Thou slept later than thou usually doth," he smiled. "Still, thou art awake before most of the servants," he joked.

"I wish thee a safe trip to London and an equally safe return," she smiled back at him and tiptoed to kiss him on the cheek.

"Farewell, my beautiful daughter." He gave her a squeeze on both arms and kissed her forehead.

A few minutes later, Joan joined her as together they waved off the procession that traveled with her father.

"What be our plan for today, my lady?" Joan asked.

"I need to go to visit Leonardo," Elizabeth said. "Alone," she added in a stern voice.

"'Twill never do," Joan insisted. "Bennet and I will go with you."

"I need to talk to him in private. I would not want the two of you to wait outside for me the whole time. Use the time to do something fun with Bennet," she teased. "We may decide to travel to Lyresham today. I learned something last night in the other realm that may solve my predicament. If I do not return by dinner, prithee, do not fret."

"I really dislike the sound of this," Joan gave her a hard sideways look.

"I will be fine, I promise. I will be with Leonardo. He will let nothing happen to me."

Joan grumbled a bit more about letting her off on her own without a chaperone, but in the end, Elizabeth got her way, as was usually the case. Joan went with Elizabeth to have the same discussion with Bennet, who, begrudgingly, ended up letting Elizabeth take Cheerio on her own. After Elizabeth was on her way, Bennet pulled Joan into his arms.

Elizabeth rode to the stream. There, she dismounted Cheerio near a shallow area. She took off her boots and used her belt to tie her cotehardie above her knees. She led Cheerio through the water and tied her to a tree on the other side. Elizabeth sat by the stream as her feet and shins dried. She had only crossed the stream one other time. It was the time she had first met Leonardo. All the other times they had met, Leonardo had come to meet her at their picnic spot by the tree with Bennet and Joan.

She let Cheerio have a drink from the stream. Then she mounted again and rode the remaining kilometer to Leonardo's home.

Leonardo's father, Matias, had commissioned a pleasant cottage for his small family nearly thirty years ago. He had brought his new bride, Maria, from Spain, to live in this rural area of England. Maria was soon pregnant with Leonardo. Two years after Leonardo's birth, Maria fell victim to pneumonia. The people of this era did not know about penicillin or its healing properties for various bacterial infections. Maria died and Matias grieved for years. After his heart had healed, Matias traveled to various parts of England. He then broadened his travels to different parts of Europe, leaving Leonardo in the care of his grandparents during his youth. Leonardo had told her one of his father's trips had even taken him as far as the New World. This was impressive given the early status of the Spanish colonization effort in North America for this era. Matias would return to check in on Leonardo every couple of years. Matias' latest trip embarked mere weeks before Elizabeth knocked on his door. According to Leonardo, this was the longest Matias had been away from their home.

Elizabeth tied Cheerio's reins to a nearby fence post. She used the knocker on the door. It was still considered fairly early in the morning in this realm. She realized she did not know Leonardo's sleeping schedule. He lived alone without a household staff, so he answered the door himself with hair mussed from sleep. His facial expression was groggy. It took him a moment to register it was Elizabeth at his door. In the meantime, she blushed and looked at the ground. He had answered the door without a shirt and wearing only his breeches.

"Elizabeth!" He was shocked as he fully awakened. "Art thou alone?" He looked around for Bennet and Joan.

"I am alone," she said. "I have great news to share with thee!" She averted her eyes as she slid by him and entered the cottage.

"Wait here," he guided her to a chair. "I will dress."

He disappeared into a nearby room. She took the opportunity to peek around the cottage. It was impeccably clean and organized. After he dressed, he found her in his laboratory.

"Leonardo, this room is magnificent!"

"Many thanks to thee. If not for the visions thou brings of the future…" he humbly responded.

"That's not true. You were already a brilliant scientist, full of theories, when I met you."

She looked over his herb garden growing in a corner that had been converted to a make-shift greenhouse. The stacks of glass panes let in lots of southern light. This was very impressive to Elizabeth because glass was not easily available to common households during this era. The knowledge he shared with the nobles must indeed compensate him well, she thought. She noted the herbs he was growing held medicinal value. He kept the small garden to help his immediate neighbors in times of need. Leonardo was a kind and caring man. He took a commission from his work, but he did not charge nearly its worth. His motivations were mainly altruistic in nature. While his genealogy spread throughout northern Spain, he had only ever known England as his home.

This was his country, and he wanted his brethren to be successful and healthy.

"I have exciting news." Elizabeth hooked her arm into his. Her words were fast and seemingly from one breath. "I had the most thrilling day with my psychiatrist, Dr. Sawyer. I will tell you all about it, but we must make haste and travel to Lyresham today. Actually, now! There is a wizard visiting. His name is Simon Fulmer. Has your father ever mentioned him or written about him?" Not waiting for him to answer, she went on. "Fulmer was called by the Greene family to entertain their autumn gala. If we get there before he moves on, he may be able to help with my condition! My father received an invitation, but he cannot attend. He has been called off to London. The parchment lists the date of the gala and it is tomorrow! Will you go with me? Today? Now?"

Leonardo had never seen Elizabeth in such an energetic state. "Yes, of course I will! Elizabeth, we must go back and retrieve Bennet and Joan. 'Twas foolish of thee to come here alone. We mustn't give thy father any reason to reject my proposal or to think it comes from anything other than love."

"Oh, decorum is so old-fashioned." She laughed at his puzzled look. "OK, let us fetch them. But they better move fast!"

Joan and Bennet were relieved to see Elizabeth return so quickly with Leonardo. They were also happy to accompany the couple to Lyresham. On the ride, Elizabeth recalled the events that had happened the day before in the future realm to her companions. They listened with rapt attention, as they did each time she told them of her experiences in the other realm.

"So you see, I might not have to await Matias' return. It is my hope that this sorcerer would be able to make me whole in this realm." She looked at her friends. Joan was obviously happy for her friend. Bennet was contemplative. Leonardo was open-mouthed and stunned.

"Tell me more about the library. How many floors did thou say there were?" he asked.

IT WAS AFTER NOON WHEN they arrived at Lyresham Hall. As Elizabeth rode on the back of Cheerio, she thought of her poor automobile waiting for her in 2015. Even in its dilapidated state, the car would have delivered them the few miles to Lyresham Hall in minutes. They rode their horses up the long entrance road. Valets were ready to take the horses, along with Bennet, to the stables. Elizabeth showed her father's invitation to the butler at the door.

"My lady, the event is not for another day and ye are not on the list for sleeping accommodations." The butler looked pointedly at their clothing. "Perhaps thou could use the time to…um…freshen up? There is a fine boarding house in town."

Asshole.

"Dear man, we have traveled here, not for the gala itself, but for a private meeting with the wizard thy mistress has hired for the event." Elizabeth was gracious and dignified despite her flushed face and undecorated riding dress. "If thou wouldst lead us to Mr. Simon Fulmer for a private conversation, we will be long gone before thy guests arrive."

The butler did not look overly convinced he should take action.

"We have also brought a gift for the hosts if they would allow us the privilege we seek." She pulled a small sack of coins from her saddlebag.

"Right this way, my lady," the butler bowed low and took the bag of coins.

The butler led them down the main hall and into a drawing room. There was a long wooden table with plenty of seating available. Joan walked over to the windows and admired the view of the gardens. She sat down and folded her hands on her lap. Of course, Leonardo and Elizabeth had no qualms perusing the many volumes of books on the shelves that lined the opposite wall. They ignored anything that was created by the printing press and paid more attention to the handwritten volumes available. They huddled together, sharing rare treasures they encountered with each other. Elizabeth wasn't expecting to find any manuscripts that would assist in her endeavor, but hope was never far from reach that she would someday stumble across a lucky gem. Such was not the case this day.

Simon Fulmer entered the room with a flourish of self-importance. Joan disliked him instantly, but as always, remained quiet. Leonardo and Elizabeth returned the manuscripts to the shelves.

"Hello," Elizabeth spoke first. "Thank you for agreeing to meet with us. I am Elizabeth Percy. This is my intended, Leonardo Navarro and my handmaiden, Joan." She was excited to meet this wizard. She stepped toward him to tell him about her dilemma. Although her recent experience with Dr. Sawyer should have eased the way for her to repeat the tale of her two lives, she still found it difficult to open up with the stranger.

"It is my pleasure to serve, my lady. How may I be of help to you today?" Simon was immediately taken by Elizabeth's pretty features. He seemed more than willing to entertain the noble girl and her companions. Leonardo sensed both Elizabeth's hesitation and Simon's immediate interest in his fiancée.

"If I may present our circumstances," Leonardo looked to Elizabeth for approval, which she gave in a nod. "We have a tricky situation which we seek a solution to. A solution we believe is magical in nature."

"Intriguing. Please tell me more," Simon continued to gaze at Elizabeth which made Leonardo uncomfortable.

"My *betrothed*…" Leonardo emphasized the word and was granted a brief glance from the wizard before he returned his leer to Elizabeth, "…hath lived her life with a great burden. It seems a spell may have been conjured at her birth, whereupon it transported Elizabeth and her mother to a futuristic realm. The transportation was not complete. She is living a simultaneous existence in this time and in the future. Her consciousness bounces between the two realms when she sleeps."

Simon had stopped looking at Elizabeth to gape in astonishment at Leonardo.

"She alternates between the timelines daily," Leonardo continued.

"Rubbish," Simon said. "Thou cometh to poke fun at my craft! To bring this incredible tale to me? To what end?" He was shouting at Leonardo.

"No, not rubbish," Leonardo replied while looking at the floor and taking a step forward. He knew how ridiculous it sounded. He looked up and met a hard stare from Simon.

Simon looked Leonardo in the eye in silence. He was expecting Leonardo to confess the prank and gave him ample time to do so.

"Is this within thy practice, sir?" Leonardo asked the wizard.

"'Tis not a trick? A jest for thee and thy noble friends to laugh about?" Simon asked.

"No, sir," Elizabeth stepped forward to speak. "My plight is real."

Again, Simon eyed Elizabeth with an inappropriate interest. Leonardo was greatly perturbed. Joan grew nervous as she watched Simon. She thought Elizabeth might not be aware of the danger in front of her. She felt Elizabeth, even with her future world knowledge, was very naïve when it came to a man's lust. Elizabeth had been fortunate to have the respectful true love she found with Leonardo.

"I shall help thee," Simon spoke slowly. The gears were turning in his mind. A plan emerged. "I have heard tell of the infliction thou speaketh of and know the spell that hast been cast. I can rectify the split in the soul and make it whole again. We will need a fifth, assuming the three of ye are also willing to take part in the spell I have in mind."

"Bennet," Joan volunteered. "I shall fetch him." She waited for Elizabeth and Leonardo to nod and then left the room to bring Bennet from the stables.

"Good to hear. We will need five people to join in a circle. When thy girl returns with this Bennet, we shall begin. Please, wait here a moment whilst I gather some herbs from my case." Simon left the room.

"What good fortune!" Elizabeth exclaimed. She wrapped her arms around Leonardo's neck, smiling up at him.

"I'm not sure we can trust this wizard," he whispered. "He hath impure thoughts when he looks at thee. 'Tis obvious to all who witness."

"That matters not," she whispered back. "So long as he can reunite the halves of my soul in this realm, I care not how he looks at me."

"Please, don't be reckless. We must be on our guard around him," Leonardo warned. He grasped her hands and brought them to his lips.

Simon returned to the room and his eyes narrowed briefly at the sight of Leonardo kissing Elizabeth's hands. Neither one noticed Simon had tumbled the lock silently when he turned to close the door.

"That was quick," Elizabeth said.

"I need little to perform what this magic," Simon smiled lasciviously at Elizabeth. "Both of you come here." He gestured to Elizabeth and Leonardo.

Elizabeth was first positioned. He lined her up, facing north on the edge of a rug. Then he motioned for Leonardo to stand next to Elizabeth.

"Which realm do you wish to exist in? Hither with your *betrothed*?" Simon asked, as he turned her head slightly.

"Here, yes," she answered. Her heart was beating faster, hoping she would never have to return to the year 2015 in Marysville, California.

"Very good. It is much easier to combine the soul in the realm of origin. Please focus your gaze on the candlestick on the mantle. Concentrate on it and do not look away."

He left Elizabeth, presumably to position Leonardo. As Elizabeth gazed unwaveringly at the candlestick, Simon deftly produced some herbs in his palm and passed them under Leonardo's nostrils. Leonardo immediately collapsed to sleep. Simon caught him and quietly lowered him to the ground. He looked up and was pleased that Elizabeth's eyes were still locked on the candlestick.

"When your friends return, we will begin the spell," he reassured her. He walked up behind her. At first, he didn't make a move. He reveled in her acquiescence. She did not break her gaze from the candlestick. Her desperation to begin the spell likely kept her from blinking. He felt his erection grow harder in anticipation.

"In the meantime," he whispered into her ear, "I am going to have my way with you."

Her blood chilled at his words, and her gaze snapped away from the candlestick to her surroundings. In an instant, she assessed he had rendered Leonardo unconscious. Simon quickly grabbed her arms and pulled her towards him. She twisted until she had her backside to him. He laughed at her squirming.

"Let me go!" she yelled.

He reached up and cupped her mouth into silence. He shuffled her over to a chair and bent her over it. She was pinned between him and the piece of furniture. She inhaled deeply through her nostrils and calmed her mind. All the self-defense training classes she had taken in the future sprang to mind. As he fumbled with the drawstring on his breeches, she brought her elbow up fast to make strong contact with his ear. He stumbled backwards while she twisted fully back around and brought her knee up swiftly to his groin. As he doubled over in pain, she did not relent. She brought her other knee up swiftly and slammed it into his nose. She ran over to the mantle and grabbed the candlestick he had made her stare at for so long.

"You bitch!" Simon yelled as blood gushed from his nose into his hands. He hurt everywhere. As he looked up to defend her next attack, the candlestick she held bashed into the side of his face. He passed out from the pain.

Elizabeth kept her wits about her. Snatching the curtain tieback from a nearby window, she tied Simon's hands behind his back. Then she hurried over to Leonardo. She checked his breathing.

"Thank goodness!" she exclaimed with relief that Leonardo was only asleep.

The handle on the door to the room turned normally and then jiggle furiously. Joan had returned with Bennet and began knocking and shouting into the room.

"Elizabeth! Leonardo! Are you there?" Joan called.

"Just a minute," Elizabeth called back. She looked down at her dress and smoothed out a place where Simon had torn it in their struggle.

She went to the door and released the lock. She opened the door. Joan and Bennet came in and their expressions quickly changed to concern when they saw the scene before them.

"I'm fine," Elizabeth assured them. "I think Leonardo is too. He is breathing. I think the wizard dosed him with something to make him sleep."

Bennet hunched over, checking the knot on Simon's wrists.

"What happened?" Joan asked.

"Simon was positioning us for the spell while we awaited your return. Suddenly, Leonardo was unconscious and Simon was trying to rape me." Elizabeth started sobbing uncontrollably.

"Oh, my dear, you are safe now," Joan threw her arms around her friend to console her.

"It's not that." Elizabeth swiped her runny nose and gulped at the air. She pulled away from Joan and stood up to pace the room. "I really..." She put her hands on her hips and looked up at the ceiling, then looked down at Leonardo, who was peacefully sleeping. She kneeled down beside him and fingered a lock of his hair. She slowly regained her composure. "I really thought Simon was a solution. I should have known it was too good to be true. Even if he could help me, he never would now. I now doubt all of his abilities anyway, after using such a cheap trick on Leonardo. It just seems so hopeless. I will never be whole."

"Please do not give up hope, my lady," Joan was near to tears herself. She placed a hand on her friend's shoulder. "With Dr. Sawyer as your new ally and his resources on the other side, you will surely locate more sorcerers from this era."

Elizabeth sighed and closed her eyes. She must admit what she did not want to.

"Joan, I am finding it increasingly difficult to believe in magic or sorcery. It is all just fables. Look at Simon. He is just a man with some herbs. He is a depraved and violent man."

"How, other than magic, would you explain your predicament?" Joan asked.

"Perhaps, I am delusional. Maybe this is all a fantastic hallucination. If it is, then I need to enjoy my dreams. Why am I chasing fraudulent men masquerading as wizards? I don't wish to have nightmares of near violence. Not when I can instead dream of our picnics by the stream and a marriage to this lovely man. None of it is real, but it is a wonderful escape."

Elizabeth looked down at Leonardo's peaceful expression as the realms shifted her existence once again. As she awoke in Marysville, California, in 2015, she could hear Joan's voice trailing off.

"I am real," she said.

5

THURSDAY, AUGUST 6, 2015 MARYSVILLE, CA

Elizabeth woke to the sounds and stench of the modern age. She did not cry this morning. She still felt the hyper-alertness which she carried over from the events at Lyresham. There was no rush to get out of bed, but she got up anyway. She still had one more day off before she returned to work and delivered an answer to Daphne about the promotion offer. The air was stale. She opened her bedroom window and the window in her living area. The parallel windows created a cross breeze throughout her tiny apartment. She could only do this in the mornings as August temperatures in California rise swiftly in the afternoons.

She went through the motions of her usual morning grooming routine. Then she sat on her small sofa with a cup of decaffeinated tea and stared off in silence around the tiny apartment. She thought about what she had told Joan.

Was it real? Was her father a 16th century nobleman? Was Leonardo real? Or was it all just dreams or delusions? Was she wasting her life in this realm?

She looked at the clock. Dr. Sawyer's office would not open for a few more hours. She grabbed her keys and decided to run some mindless errands.

First, she went to the grocery store and pushed a small cart around for an hour. She thought about all the things she had talked about with Dr. Sawyer the day before. She decided she would accept the promotion and enroll in night courses at Yuba College. This way, she could keep her job and her apartment for the time being. It would be a smaller transition than uprooting everything to move to Sacramento. The tuition was lower at the local college than at the state university. She wondered what college would be like. She never attended public schools. When she lived at Marlowe, several teachers worked at the hospital. Her classwork was akin to a homeschooled student. When she was eighteen, she attained her GED certification. She also took the college placement exams and was told that she had scored well. She thought about the different areas of study that were available in this era.

When she returned to her apartment, she spotted Noah walking to his car. He shifted his backpack and quickly jogged over to help Elizabeth carry her groceries.

"Noah, just the person I wanted to see," she said.

"Really?" His face lit up with a bright smile.

"Yes," she laughed. "My uncle, who you met yesterday, well, he talked me into gaining a higher education."

"That's great! Are you enrolling at Cal State this fall?"

"No, I think I will start here at Yuba College. I was

wondering what you could tell me about the campus, the curriculum and….well, everything." She unlocked her apartment door, and they brought the bags to the counter. Her choice of matriculation clearly disappointed him.

"I'm headed to work right now, but I'm free tonight," he peeked into one of her bags. "You could invite me over for dinner." He looked inside one bag. "I like yogurt, frozen entrees and let me see," he rooted around in the bag.

"How rude!" she teased him. She snatched the bag away as he lifted a canister.

"Oh, yes, oatmeal is my favorite." He winked at her.

"OK, you can come over. Around five?"

"Five sounds perfect. See you then."

He left quickly. Elizabeth appreciated he took the time to help her carry the groceries. She guessed, based on his quick departure, that his act of kindness had likely made him late for his shift. She had just finished putting away her groceries when her mobile phone started ringing. It was always startling when that happened. There were few people who even knew her number. Those few people rarely called.

"Hello."

"Hello, Miss Percy. This is Tina from Dr. Sawyer's office. Dr. Sawyer would like a follow-up with you today. Are you free?"

"Yes."

"Dr. Sawyer has an opening in about thirty minutes. Will that time work for you?"

"Yes, that's great! I will be right over! Thank you!"

Liz gathered up the books she had borrowed with Dr.

Sawyer's credentials. As she parked her own vehicle, she noticed his car parked two spaces down the row. She recalled being a passenger in the car the day before. Her adventure at Lyresham with Leonardo, Joan and Bennet made it feel like their trip to CSUS had happened much longer ago. She paused to look at his car for a few minutes and think about the time they spent together on the drive to the CSUS library. It had felt so freeing to have a confidant in this realm. What a difference a day can make. She walked into the office building. Her wait was a short one before she was called into Dr. Sawyer's office.

"Hello," she smiled at him.

"Hello," he smiled back. "I believe this is the first time you have entered my office without shooting daggers at me with your eyes."

"I do feel a lot less hostility towards you now."

He pointed at the recorder on his desk.

"Do you consent to being on the record today?" he asked.

"Yes, of course. I have not changed my mind about that. I feel it has lifted an enormous weight since I opened up to you." She sat in a chair near his desk as he started the recording. "So long as a trip to Marlowe is not in my future, I will tell you everything."

"I promise you I do not see any reason for a patient with your symptoms to be committed. You should not have spent one night there. I want to talk to you about that later. How did you sleep last night?" he asked.

"Same as always," she smiled. "I feel rested, but I experienced a day in the other realm in the time that I should have been sleeping in my bed here."

"Can you tell me what happened in the other realm?" he asked.

"After you left me, yesterday, I read about a wizard who lived in my other time. It was in one of the books I borrowed under your name at the library we visited. That reminds me, here, I brought them back for you to return." She rummaged through her bag and placed the volumes on his desk.

"You read them all already?" he asked with an eyebrow arched.

"No, and I won't need to. You see, the wizard was a fraud. He had some herbs and cheap theatrics to fool his audiences. I would guess all wizards of lore operated the same way. They fooled people into positions of power and collected as much gold as they could trick out of their patrons. I don't think there is real magic at any time. I should have known better. Even some of the neighboring families believe Leonardo has inherited his father's talents because of some scientific advances I have shared with him."

"This is quite a different view than you presented yesterday," Dr. Sawyer came around his desk and sat in the chair opposite Liz.

"I feel different," Liz paused.

Dr. Sawyer didn't press her.

"Can I get you a cup of tea?" he asked.

"Yes, that would be lovely. Decaf or herbal if you have it."

He picked up this desk phone and pressed the button to ring Tina. He asked for two cups of chamomile tea. Then he turned to face her again.

"You feel different from yesterday? Because of your

experience last night?" he asked.

"All the time I was in the other realm last night, I thought of my conversation with you. I thought about all the conversations I have had with other doctors as well. What if they were right? What if the other world wasn't real? What if I am delusional? The simplest answer is often the correct one, right?"

Tears were sliding down her cheeks. Dr. Sawyer picked up a box of tissues and passed them to her. After she dabbed a bit, she took a deep breath. There was a light knock at the door. Dr. Sawyer jumped up to receive a tea tray from Tina. He brought it to his desk. He poured a cup for Liz and handed it to her. She took a sip.

"If I am delusional, how do you fix me?" she asked.

"For a patient experiencing delusional behavior, the best course of action is exactly what you are doing. There isn't a pill you can take as a solution. Someone should only prescribe medication when delusions are affecting social or occupational functions. Hospitalization is a huge mistake in treating delusions, as you well know. You should focus on bettering your life in this realm. Go to college. Have a rewarding career. Make new friends. In short, the best thing you can do is live this life as best you can. Over time, if you tip the scales to this side, then the other life becomes less significant."

"What you are saying sounds logical. I suppose it wouldn't hurt to implement a few of your suggestions as an experiment," she said.

"I think we should continue to see each other once a week. Remember, you can tell me anything. We should be honest with each other. I will tell you now that I believe they have mishandled your condition in the past. I know that you have taken part in a sleep study before, but would you be willing to do it again, under my direction? Recent technological advances may detect a physiological symptom during your sleep."

"Sure."

"Great! We will schedule that with Tina before you leave. Now, let's talk about your interests. Together, we should be able to come up with at least one thing you can do in a social setting."

They filled the remainder of her session by discussing her decision to go to college. She decided she would enter with an undeclared major. When she told him she would take the promotion Daphne had offered and go to school at night, he asked that she consider a four-year program and live on campus amongst others her age. She left his office feeling that her opportunities were endless.

She thought about her decisions all afternoon. It was less than a month before fall semester started. Applications were past due, so she would need to complete them quickly. She looked around her tiny apartment and couldn't imagine a dormitory room could be much smaller. She would have a roommate if she followed that path. Perhaps a roommate would be good for her. She had heard many tales of long-lasting friendships igniting at university between roommates. She wondered if they would match her with a girl like Joan. Thoughts of Joan led to thoughts of Leonardo. These were the people she held most dear to her heart. Is it possible that they were figments of my imagination? Would they fade away with time?

After leaving Dr. Sawyer's office, she had stopped by the grocery store again to pick up a pre-cooked rotisserie chicken for dinner with Noah. While she daydreamed of college, she carved chunks of the meat onto two plates of spinach and sprinkled some grated parmesan on top. Then she wrapped the two plates and refrigerated them. Her apartment was already tidy, but she spent a little time dusting and vacuuming. It was the first time she was having company in her home and she wanted her space to be comfortable and clean. She used the rest of the afternoon to read a book in between loads of laundry at the complex's onsite laundromat.

Noah arrived a few minutes after five. Liz had seen him walking over through her courtyard-facing window, but suddenly he turned back and returned to his apartment. Then a few minutes later, he re-emerged with a small box in his hand. Liz opened the door to him before he could knock.

"Hi, I'm so glad you could come tonight." She was warm and welcoming.

"I brought a movie." He held up the box. It was a popular science fiction thriller based on a book she had read somewhat recently.

"Oh, I don't think I have a way to play a movie," she explained as she waved her hand around her living room. Even with her store discount, she could not see the value in owning a television. "And I don't think I could stay up late enough to watch it. I go to sleep pretty early."

"That's ok. Some other time I will talk you into coming to my place to watch it."

He left the movie on the counter and followed her

short trek to the small multi-purpose table with two chairs. It surprised him to see the chicken salads. They sat at the table and talked about Yuba College, California State University in Sacramento, and some other nearby institutions. He was clearly nudging her towards CSUS. He told her that CSUS was having an open house this weekend and he would be happy to take her on a tour. The time passed quickly as they chatted about tuition, student loans, books, and student clubs. When Liz yawned, Noah took his cue to leave.

"Thank you for all the information you shared tonight about your experience at Yuba. I think I would like to go to the open house at CSUS. Let me see if I can switch my schedule at work to have the day off." She walked him to the door.

"May I see your cell phone?" he asked.

She handed it to him and he programmed his number.

"Text me when you know," he opened the door to leave. "Liz, I really enjoyed tonight. Thank you for dinner."

Liz watched through the window as he walked around the railing to his side of the courtyard and entered his apartment. She locked her door, closed the window and drew the curtains. As she walked back to get ready for bed, she saw the movie on the counter. She wondered if he left it on purpose as an excuse to come back for it. She smiled.

6

HADLEIGH, SUFFOLK, ENGLAND - 1555

Elizabeth woke in the dark to the familiar smells of a musty manor, but not her home. She was a little surprised. Not that she was in a guest bedroom of Lyresham Hall, but given her epiphanies in the other realm the day before with Dr. Sawyer, she half expected this world to vanish into the deep recesses of her brain. Maybe Dr. Sawyer was right and it would fade with time as she increased her quality of life in the future realm.

She sat up in the bed as the events of the previous day in this realm flooded her memory. After she had thwarted the so-called wizard's attempt to rape her, Joan and Bennet had sat on the floor with her next to Leonardo's sleeping form. As the butler passed by the drawing room, it outraged him to see Simon trussed up and unconscious. His demeanor changed quickly when he was told of the attack. He called for the footmen to come and restrain the wizard. He also sent for the local constable. An attack on a noblewoman would not go unpunished. A footman searched Simon's pockets and was soon lying on the floor next to Leonardo in a deep sleep after he discovered the herbal anesthetic Simon had pocketed.

Leonardo had woken a few hours later. He had been too groggy to travel, so the butler had arranged with the Duchess of Lyresham to give them rooms for the night. Duchess Mary Vaughan had been quite cross about the attack and cared nothing for losing a magical performance for her gala that evening. She demanded that they jail Simon in the small dungeon on premises. She took a private dinner with Elizabeth and hailed her bravery and actions. Mary asked Elizabeth if she would be willing to teach herself and some other noblewomen the same maneuvers that had saved her maidenhood. Elizabeth responded she was more than willing to share her skills with any interested women, be they of noble descent or common birth. Mary was grateful and offered to host the classes discreetly at Lyresham. The ladies bade each other good night.

And now Elizabeth was awake in a strange bedroom. She dressed in the dark and peeked out into the hallway. She made her way to the banquet room, where servants were already filling tables with fruits and pastries. The house guests for the ball that evening would arrive soon. Joan joined her not long after. Bennet followed soon after Joan. Perhaps a bit too soon, Elizabeth smiled. She never pried into Joan and Bennet's love affair, but she had the impression that their intimacy breached what was considered proper for this era.

Leonardo was the last to arrive. He was angry. His clothing was disheveled, as if he had dressed as quickly and minimally as possible. He was carrying his outer jacket and hat. When he found Elizabeth in the banquet room, he rushed over and wrapped his arms around her. He buried his face in her hair and held her tightly.

"How art thou?" he asked.

"I am fine, are you?" she asked.

"No!" he shouted. "I woke up this morning, and a footman told me about yesterday's events. Is he still alive, or did they behead him immediately?"

"I don't think he is going to be beheaded. They jailed him for the moment. The constable will take him for judgment and punishment. He was unsuccessful in his attack. I'm not sure what the punishment will be for the attempt." Elizabeth extracted herself from his tight embrace and held his hands. She walked him over to a chair and motioned for him to sit. He sat and scowled.

"Let's have some of this food and be on our way. I am sure the Lord and Lady of Lyresham have enough to do today without worrying if we are going to impose on their ball." She tucked some of Leonardo's unkempt hair behind his ear in a tender gesture. "I'm fine," she reassured him.

They ate quickly and waited outside as Bennet and Joan brought around the horses. Lady Mary stepped out to see them off. She assured Leonardo that justice would be sought for Simon's actions and she would send word of the proceedings to Lady Elizabeth's estate.

When they arrived at Elizabeth's land, they rode on to their secluded spot next to the stream on the south border. Bennet gave chase to Joan in the woods so that Leonardo and Elizabeth could have a private moment. They sat quietly on the grass near the stream. Elizabeth told Leonardo of the decisions she had made in the other realm. She told him she was still undecided as to a four-year university or the local community college. He encouraged her to pursue the university and beyond. He agreed with Dr. Sawyer. She should build as good a life as she could on the other side.

"I was thinking of something else while in the other realm yesterday," she said.

"Oh?" he asked.

"I was thinking about what is real. When Simon attacked me, I understood in that instant what others perceive as magic in this realm is only trickery. People like him use herbs and chemical reactions to fool the inexperienced minds. There is no such thing as real magic. Then I wondered if I really am delusional? Did I create this world as an escape from the orphanage when I was young? Is all my Internet research on this era fueling my dreams at night?" she asked.

Leonardo sat staring at the stream. He took a moment to contemplate what was real. In his youth, he had seen his father perform great magic. There was no scientific explanation for all he had witnessed. He plucked a wildflower from the ground nearby. He feathered it against her cheek.

"Doth thou feel this? Doth thou smell it?" he moved it beneath her nose.

"I don't know if I can trust my sense of touch and smell to tell me what is real," she replied.

He leaned over and kissed her.

"Is this real?" he asked, pulling away.

"No, this is, most decidedly, the best dream ever," she pulled him back into the kiss. Leonardo boldly ran his hand up her dress and along her inner thigh.

Suddenly, there was a crack of lightning on the ground next to them, accompanied by a thunderous roar. A man stepped clear of the smoke cloud that filled the area.

"Stop!" the man yelled.

The man was of average height with thick brown shaggy hair that was flecked with gray. He wore functional peasant's clothing and looked as if he had not bathed in quite some time. He focused his gaze on Elizabeth. She could see beneath the dirt and scruff was a handsome Spaniard who had green eyes freckled with gold and thick, dark lashes.

"Father?" Leonardo asked.

Leonardo's father, Matias Navarro, came into full view as he and Elizabeth broke their embrace and stood up. Matias rummaged through the bag he wore at his hip and pulled out a pin. He walked over to Elizabeth and snatched up her hand. Before she realized what was happening, he pricked her finger.

"Ouch!" she squealed and snatched back her hand. He snatched it back and muttered some indistinguishable and foreign language she had never heard before. He held her pricked finger up and gently blew on it. The droplet of blood that had pooled floated into the air. He then pricked his own finger and blew a droplet of his blood into the air to meet hers. The droplets repelled each other. He then snagged Leonardo's hand and performed the same puncture. He blew Leonardo's blood over toward the other two droplets. Leonardo's blood repelled Elizabeth's. It was instead attracted to Matias' droplet and when the two droplets made contact, they mixed. Matias let out a sigh. He looked at the two young people.

"You may carry on," he grumbled and placed his pin in his bag. He turned his back to them and walked toward his home.

"Wait!" Elizabeth shouted. "Did you just do a hocus pocus DNA test on me?" She ran over and grabbed his arm. He turned to look at her. He had a deep, soulful sadness in his expression.

"Dee-en-ay?" Matias asked. "What say you, girl?" He moved to leave again.

"What was that? With our blood? What did you do?" she asked, standing in his path.

"Thou art the image of thy mother," he stood looking at her.

"Father?" Leonardo put his hand on Matias' shoulder. His father seemed so old and frail compared to the last time he saw him. "How art thou?"

Matias remained silent as he gazed upon Elizabeth. His eyes welled up. He swiped his tears away and sat on the ground. Elizabeth and Leonardo sat next to him. Elizabeth was empathetic to the man's sadness, although she had yet to know the reason for his tears.

"I will tell thee." Matias looked over at Elizabeth again. "I will tell thee everything. I sensed thy impending union and transported myself as fast as I could. I used thy blood to determine if thou art a familial match for Leonardo and myself in order to prevent an incestuous relationship. Thou art not a blood relation to us."

"Why would you think so?" she asked without really wanting to know the answer that was blatantly obvious.

"I love her. Katharine." He sobbed. "She loves me

too. She loves thy father, of course. But she loves me too."

Matias buried his face in his hands.

"And now she's gone and I am the one to blame," he muttered.

Elizabeth's eyes widened.

"I won't pretend to absolve you of your apparent intrusion into a happy marriage," she said. "But you are not to blame for my mother's death."

"She's not dead!" he shouted. "I can't find whence I put her."

He stood up. Elizabeth rose as well. Matias looked as if he were going to leave as abruptly and mystically as he had arrived. He and Elizabeth looked into each other's eyes for a moment. Both seemed to make the connection at the same time.

"Tell me thy story, girl," Matias demanded.

"You tell me yours first," Elizabeth leveled her glare at him. "What did you do?"

"Mmmm, thou art a bold girl. Alright then, let's sit again." They sat. Leonardo flushed. He had never known of his father's affair with Katharine. Joan and Bennet came running from a nearby patch of trees to see what the commotion was all about. Elizabeth introduced them to Matias and encouraged him to speak in front of them as well.

"My love affair with Katharine started right hither. 'Tis such a romantic spot. We would meet hither often and have picnics under that tree and listen to the water trickle." He pointed to a large tree near the bank of the stream.

"When the birth of Katharine's child was near term, I

performed a spell that convinced us I was the father of the child she carried. I must have muddled that up as well…" He sighed and looked up at the sky. "We didn't want to bring heartache to your father. We just wanted to raise our child together. I found some scrolls that spoke of a spell that could move a person to a distinct part of the world. I performed the spell to move my love, Katharine and my blood, the child she was carrying, or so I thought, to the New World discovered by the Spaniards. She was in such pain as the birthing process began. I held her hand as I delivered the spell. She vanished before my eyes, yet the babe remained. I could hear the birthing ladies whom the servants had called for coming down the hall. I tried the spell again, but it had nary an effect on thee. I had to leave thee for the birthing ladies to discover and care for whilst I looked for Katharine. I worried for her physically and emotionally, not knowing how having a babe magically removed from the body would affect her being. I had to find her and make sure she knew our baby was alive and healthy. I have since transported myself to the New World many times, but I cannot find her anywhere. The land is incredibly vast and the Spanish are claiming more territories each day. I looked…" he trailed off. He looked up at Elizabeth. "I am so very sorry. I lost her."

Elizabeth had been told in this realm that her mother had abandoned her moments after her birth. And now, she looked over at the frail man, who was openly sobbing. He was so thin. Leonardo was also looking at his father. The older man was nearly unrecognizable to him. Matias was gaunt and the volume of emotion he displayed today was so unlike his character. Leonardo had never seen him like this.

"It doesn't matter *where* you look for her," Elizabeth began. "It matters *when*."

"What doth thou mean, child?" Matias looked hopeful.

"It is my turn to tell you my story. I never knew how, but it must have been your spell. It transported my mother and myself to the New World. To a place called Sacramento, California."

"Thou wast left hither. Thou art hither. The spell did not transport thee." He eyed her suspiciously.

"My mother and I were transported into the *future*. The spell did not work wholly on me. A part of my soul was left here at this time, in this body. Another part was sent with my mother and born into another body."

"That is not possible. I was very specific about what was to be transported, my blood and my love. If thou art not my blood relation, which thou art not, then nary a particle of thee would move with the spell. I did not create another body for thee in this realm nor in the New World. I have not the knowledge to complete such an action." He was quite confident. "The time travel…how far into the future?" Matias asked.

"The year I was born in Sacramento was 1995." Elizabeth answered.

"'Tis too far. I shall not live to see her again lest I too can travel to the future. I can figure that out. If I…" He was lost in thought and making gestures in the air.

"My mother died soon after she arrived in the future." Elizabeth reached over to hold his hand, which abandoned its gesticulations upon hearing the words that Katharine was dead. "She had a difficult labor and bled out. The medical team from the future could not save her in time. Telling you her chances of survival were much better in the future than they would have been here is little consolation, I know."

"She is gone?" he whispered. "She is really gone?"

"Yes," Elizabeth replied.

"How doth thou know this? Explain what thou meant when thou described, only part of thy soul was transported," he demanded.

Elizabeth told him of her life experiencing two realms simultaneously. She described the switch that happened when she went to sleep in either place. She told him of the missing blocks of time and how they would catch up to her the next morning when she would wake in this realm because of the sleep schedule and the differing time zones.

"Twins," he muttered.

"What?" Elizabeth and Leonardo both asked.

"There were two babies! How did I not know! I didn't muddle the spell so much. Katharine was carrying two babies! One was mine!" Matias was euphoric.

Elizabeth was reeling at the possibility. *Could it be? No, of course not.* She was confident she was the same person in both realms.

"It cannot be possible," Leonardo spoke up. "As I understand, if one man impregnates a woman, she cannot be impregnated again, correct?"

"It is possible. I have read about it," Elizabeth said. She covered her face with her hands and mumbled through them. "It is possible in humans, and more common in animals. I forget what it is called."

Both men were silent as they looked at Elizabeth. Her

mind was racing. She peeked through her hands at the position of the sun. It was nearing the time that she would wake up in the other realm. *Was it possible?* She thought about the slight differences in her appearance in the other realm. Her hair color. Her eye color. She looked at Leonardo's loving face. She looked into his green and gold eyes and she knew…

7

FRIDAY, AUGUST 7, 2015 MARYSVILLE, CA

"No!" Liz screamed when she woke up.

"No!" she screamed again.

She jumped out of the bed and stepped over to the bathroom. She looked in the mirror. There wasn't enough light. Her hand quickly slapped the light switch behind her to the "on" position. The thin fluorescent tube above her medicine cabinet slowly hummed and flickered until it achieved maximum brightness. She leaned over the sink and looked at her eyes closely in the mirror.

"No," she whispered.

Her eyes were the same as Leonardo's, green with gold specks. She stood there, frozen, in front of the mirror, staring at her own eyes. She wasn't sure how much time had passed with her standing like that. When she saw the tears running down her face, she punched the mirror.

The broken mirror cut her hand, and it was now bleeding. She wrapped a hand towel around it as she left the bathroom and sat at her table. She shuddered.

"Leonardo," she cried. "Leonardo is my brother."

She looked at the clock. It would be hours before Dr. Sawyer would be in his office. She looked at the calendar on the wall. It was Friday. She was supposed to go to work on Fridays. She was supposed to give Daphne an answer today about the promotion.

"Leonardo is my brother," she repeated. "I kissed him."

She turned in her chair and looked back toward her bedroom. She should shower. She should get dressed. She looked at the towel covering her hand. The wound was bleeding through. She would have to deal with the cut before anything else. She tried to calm herself with breathing.

"Leonardo is my brother." The same words came to her over and over. They slid around her mind repeatedly like a tornado about to swallow her consciousness.

"His hand was on my thigh." She realized they had been on the cusp of taking their relationship to the next level.

She gently pulled the towel away from her hand. Blood oozed out and dripped on her pajama pants. Winding the towel around tightly, she pinched it with her thumb against her palm. The pain was intense, but it wasn't enough to stop her thoughts. She rose to pick up her cell phone and her car keys with her free hand.

"Leonardo is my brother. We were going to get married." she stood still.

"No, you idiot!" She snapped at herself and shook her head. "He was going to marry her! He probably IS going to marry her!"

She dropped her cell phone and keys and ran to the toilet to vomit. After the dry-heaves subsided, she walked back out to her living room. Sitting in her chair at her little table again, she thought of the sleeping aids in her cabinet. She thought she should take some and go back to the other realm. She wanted to know more, but she knew it didn't work that way.

"Maybe Matias is wrong. Maybe there is another explanation." She wound her fingers through some tufts of hair and propped her elbows on the table.

"It isn't real," she whispered.

"Leonardo isn't my brother?" she asked herself hopefully.

"No, you idiot, idiot, idiot!" she callously responded. "There is no Leonardo! There never was! This is all part of your delusion!"

She stood up again, grabbed her keys and cell phone, and was out the door before she could change her mind. When she arrived at Dr. Sawyers' office building, his car was not there. She sat on the parking block for the spot his car had been parked at the day before and waited for him. While she waited, she called Daphne to say she was sick and could not work today. She couldn't remember ever doing that before. Then she tapped the internet browser icon on her cell phone. She spent the next hour waiting for Dr. Sawyer and learning about "superfecundation".

Superfecundation occurs when two egg cells in the mother are fertilized within the same cycle by two different sperm donors. The fertilization instances are within hours or days of each other and the offspring thus share the same mother, but different fathers. The offspring are referred to as dizygotic twins.

When Philip arrived at his workplace, he wasn't expecting anyone to be sitting in his parking space. It startled him when he saw Liz and he slammed on his brakes. She jumped up and stepped away from the parking block so he could pull his car in all the way. Philip took in her appearance. She had unruly hair, was still in her pajamas, and was holding her injured hand with a blood-soaked towel around it. He exited his car as fast as he could.

"Liz? Are you alright? What happened to your hand?" he asked.

"Leonardo is my brother," she said. Her eyes were wide, and she was breathing deeply and rapidly through her nose.

"Leonardo is your brother," he repeated. He led her into his office building. He offered her a seat near the reception area and went to Tina's desk to grab the first aid kit. Tina had not noticed Liz in the parking lot as she usually entered the building from another entrance. She stepped toward Philip and Liz as they approached. She looked at Philip inquisitively and he shook his head "no". He knew Tina was offering to call the police in their unspoken language. It was protocol when a patient came to the office in a distressed state and there was reason to believe the patient was a threat to themselves or others.

"Liz?" Liz looked up at him. "I am going to treat your wound. First, I want to know, do you have any weapons on your person?"

Liz looked at him in confusion.

"Oh!" she exclaimed. "Oh, no. No, I do not have any

weapons. I was upset, and I punched the mirror in my apartment. I don't have a knife or a razor or anything."

"Punched a mirror, huh?" he spoke quietly and tenderly as he kneeled in front of her and gently removed the towel from her hand. It was very sticky, as some of the blood had congealed. He used some of the dry spots on the towel to wipe away the excess blood around the cut. "I don't think you will need stitches, but we should clean this so it doesn't become infected."

He led her over to a bathroom and helped her wash and dry the cut. He used the products in the first aid kit to apply some antibiotic and bandages. While he worked, she talked.

"I visited the other realm again in my sleep. Joan, Bennet, Leonardo and I rode back to Hadleigh together after the situation with Simon Fulmer had been dealt with. We stopped at the stream I told you about. Matias, Leonardo's father, magically appeared. He told us a story of an affair he had with my mother."

Liz told him as much as she had learned before waking up in Marysville, as well as her curbside research on superfecundation. With her wounds treated, he led her back to sit in his office. Her latest episode had left her in shock. He thought she was lucky to have made the twenty-minute drive without incident.

"Why did you hit the mirror?" he asked.

"I don't know how I could have missed what was so obvious the last few years. How often have I looked into his eyes? His eyes," she looked up at Dr. Sawyer. "His eyes are the same as mine, here. Not the same as mine there, but the same as mine here. We all have our fathers' eyes. All three of us. Elizabeth from there, she has Richard's eyes. Leonardo and myself, we have Matias' eyes. Leonardo and I have the same eyes."

She was rambling and crying. Dr. Sawyer passed her some tissues and silently waited for her to calm. As the tears subsided, she noticed her pajama bottoms. She pinched some of the fabric with a bloodstain in disbelief. An awareness slowly dawned on her and she wondered what Dr. Sawyer thought of her actions this morning. Her cheeks blushed in shame. She had rushed out of her apartment in her sleepwear and barefoot, leaving a trail of blood. Her eyes looked up to meet Dr. Sawyer, who looked upon her with compassion.

"I'm so embarrassed."

"Don't be. This is not a setback, like you may be thinking. This is progress."

"I don't think so, Dr. Sawyer. Yesterday, I told you I might believe that I was having delusions. Today, I'm not so sure." She blew her nose, gathered up all the used tissues, and tossed the lot in the trash receptacle near his desk.

"This is all a part of the healing process. Your mind is trying to reconcile what is real. At some point, you will come to a conclusion. What is or has happened in Hadleigh, either it will be real to you or not. You don't have to force it. Your beliefs are your own. No one is rushing you to make a decision either way. I am here for you to talk to anytime you need it. That being said, you have physically harmed yourself today by punching the mirror. You have also put others in danger by driving while in a state of shock. I cannot ignore those actions."

"Are you going to commit me?" she stood up, panicked.

"No, no, here sit," he spoke softly and guided her back to her seat. "Your condition is a very far cry from ever needing that sort of treatment. You should never have endured that sort of treatment in the first place. Let me get back to that." he walked to his desk and opened a drawer. "What I meant was, you don't need to wait until business hours to contact me." He handed her a card. "I have a phone service for after hours. If you call my office during non-business hours, our phones forward to this service. If you like, you can call this number directly." he pointed to a secondary number on the card. "You just input your number and I am notified immediately. Here is another card," he handed her a second. "Keep one in your wallet and one in your apartment. If you feel like this again, just call me. Don't leave in haste, just call me. OK?"

Liz nodded her head. She sat quietly, holding the two cards. She had not brought her wallet with her.

"Leonardo is my brother," she had stated it many times in his presence that morning. She finally felt the need to talk about what that meant to her. "I feel so much shame. I fell in love with him with Elizabeth. I kissed him with her. I shared all of their experiences together. He was about to make love with her when his father, our father, arrived. What if he hadn't come when he did? I would never be able to erase that experience. And now that we all have this big revelation, how can I stop seeing them? Will this shared experience keep her away from him? Will they still get married? Will I share their marriage? Their children?"

She was breathing harder and felt the tears welling up in her eyes again.

"Or is it all part of the delusion working itself out in my mind? My mind could be helping me to get over Leonardo and move on with my life in this realm. Perhaps, by accepting that he is my brother, I can let go of the one thing that was holding me there in that time and place each night."

"We can only wait and see," he assured her. "As your mind determines what is real and what is not, you will have your answer."

"Thank you, Dr. Sawyer."

She turned around to look for her car keys. She found them on the side table next to the chair. As she reached for them, he stopped her.

"Don't go just yet. I have news for you," he said.

"Yes?"

"I have reviewed your files from Marlowe several times over the past few years. In the past few days, since you have confided in me, I have revisited those records. I have had calls with the institution and the Family Services department. You should never have been placed in a psychiatric facility for your condition. Nor should you have received the treatments and medications that you did. You were an orphan. The paperwork was easier to commit you than to find a suitable foster situation. Your condition required a foster home and a caseworker who would nurture you and facilitate out-patient psychiatric sessions."

Liz stared at him, aghast.

"The administration at Marlowe Psychiatric Hospital knew this. Their self-serving goal was to fill beds and collect the state funds allotted for your care. I have since brought this injustice to the District Attorney. She has

been collecting evidence to bring a case against
Marlowe Psychiatric Hospital for quite some time.
Marlowe will be assigned oversight by the state of
California to ensure this kind of mistake doesn't happen
in the future. There will be a settlement. It will be
enough for you to go to any university you like."

He went to his desk and pulled out a packet of papers.
He handed them over to her. She looked through them.
The packet contained applications for CSUS enrollment,
grants, scholarships and loans. She looked up at him.

"I don't know what to say," she said. "I don't know
which is harder to imagine. Going to college, or finding
out my birth father is a powerful sorcerer."

They laughed a little together. She reached out and
squeezed his hand.

"If you want to get into CSUS this fall, I can help you.
I have contacts there who would be happy to help. I
don't blame you if you want to go someplace
more…prestigious. I have seen your SAT scores. You
won't have any admission problems wherever you
choose to go. Since it is so late in the summer, it might
be tough, which is why I am offering to help you get into
Cal State if you would like."

"Thank you," she said. "Thank you for everything."

"You are most welcome," he said.

Dr. Sawyer helped Liz to her car and watched her
drive off.

LIZ PARKED AT HER apartment building. She felt
fortunate to be able to sneak back into her home without
bumping into any of her neighbors in her disheveled
state. She took a long hot shower while being careful not

to wet her bandages. After she dressed and dried her hair, she started the tedious process of completing the stack of paperwork Dr. Sawyer had given her. She put Leonardo and the revelation of a sister out of her mind.

An hour later, there was a knock at the door. The night before, Noah had left a movie disc on the counter. She assumed he had left it intentionally as an excuse to stop by today to retrieve it. She grabbed it and went to answer the door. When she opened the door, she dropped the movie and gasped.

Matias stood in her entryway. He grasped her hand and pricked it quickly. He then pricked his own and watched as the blood droplets rose to meet each other in midair. The droplets blended together and emitted a shining light.

"Hello, my daughter," he said. "How I have longed to meet you."

PSYCHIATRIC ASSESSMENT
From the office of Dr. Philip Sawyer

Date of Consultation: TUESDAY, *AUGUST 4, 2015*
  Consulting Physician: Dr. Philip Sawyer, M.D.
  Patient: Elizabeth Percy
  Identification: Patient is a 20-year-old female.
  Presenting Complaint(s): None
  History of Present Illness: Patient was transferred to
my care on out-patient basis two years ago. Patient
maintains delusions have stopped.
  Current Medications: None prescribed.
  Personal History: Single. No children. No significant
other. No immediate family.
  Family History: Unknown
  Mental Status Examination: Patient continues to
exhibit artifacts of delusional behavior. Her dialect often
slips to mid-sixteenth century and she continues to speak
with an English accent. She still insists her delusions
have stopped. Per her lab results, I believe she is
inducing a sleep state each night to continue the delusion
of her alternate life. She expresses anger each time I

refer to her past delusions as "dreams". During today's visit, patient was quick to dismiss the idea of a romantic involvement with a neighbor. Patient will be attending a social function with neighbors of her apartment complex. This is the first social situation she has described in session. Patient continues to be uninterested in furthering any academic pursuits. She claims to be content with simple life.

Laboratory Data: Weekly tests consistently show patient is using (perhaps abusing) melatonin and non-prescription sleep aids.

Diagnosis:

Axis I: Possible delusional disorder

Axis II: None

Axis III: None

Axis IV: Patient is attending a social event tonight (BBQ with neighbors). Will follow up - next visit.

Axis V: Current Global Assessment of Functioning rated at 61-70. Showing improvement in social functioning.

Recommendation and Plan: Pending an inspection of the patient's home, I will recommend out-patient visits to become less frequent. Patient has demonstrated financial responsibility and a good work ethic. Patient is not a threat to herself or others. Decreasing the frequency of visits may promote trust in our relationship and open communications. Patient was noticeably pleased at the suggestion. Message left for Dr. Arthur Riley regarding the patient's session recordings and sleep studies from Marlowe. Meeting scheduled with Pearl Goodwin (social worker) tomorrow afternoon to discuss patient's history of foster care. Investigation is open with CMHSOAC regarding wrongful institutionalization practices at Marlowe.

PSYCHIATRIC ASSESSMENT
From the office of Dr. Philip Sawyer

Date of Consultation: WEDNESDAY, *AUGUST 5, 2015*

Consulting Physician: Dr. Philip Sawyer, M.D.

Patient: Elizabeth Percy

Identification: Patient is a 20-year-old female.

Presenting Complaint(s): Active delusions nightly.

History of Present Illness: Patient experiencing delusional behavior since childhood. Behavior denied to physicians for three years (age 17 to 20).

Current Medications: None

Personal History: Single. No children. No significant other. No immediate family.

Family History: Unknown

Mental Status Examination: Today's session began with an onsite inspection of the patient's apartment. After confirming OTC medications in her medicine cabinet: melatonin, antihistamines, GABA, as well as documented evidence of continued delusions, I offered the patient a chance to confide off the record. OTR, the patient opened up and described the delusions that continue to occur on a nightly basis. Later, the patient granted permission for this information to be included in her permanent psychiatric record. Patient described life experience that occurs each night she goes to sleep. In her delusion, she is the daughter of a nobleman living in rural England in the mid 1500s. She spends her free time researching sorcery from the 16th century. She believes a magic spell could unite her separate existences into one version of herself. She prefers the delusional existence in the 16th century. Patient is adamant against suicide. She believes in death she will no longer exist in either world, citing her mother's death in this world as proof. She describes a romance with Leonardo, the son of a renowned sorcerer named Matias. This relationship prohibits any romantic attachment in real life. In her delusion, she has friends, family, and is in love. In real life, she is an orphan with little social interaction with others.

Laboratory Data: N/A

Diagnosis:

Axis I: Grandiose Delusional Disorder

Axis II: Symptom could lead to schizophrenia

Axis III: None

Axis IV: Offered promotion opportunity as manager at retail job

Axis V: Current Global Assessment of Functioning rated at 61-70. Little impact to social or occupational functioning.

Recommendation and Plan: Since the patient has confessed what was long suspected, treatment will continue as out-patient. Session frequency may decrease as indicated in previous session to ease the fears the patient has regarding institutionalization. Future sessions will explore and further detail the experience of the patient's delusions. As described thus far, patient only experiences delusions in sleep. As delusions do not impact patient's waking hours negatively, no medication is recommended at this time. Sessions will provide a baseline for delusions to ensure any future symptoms of schizophrenia are addressed.

PSYCHIATRIC ASSESSMENT
From the office of Dr. Philip Sawyer

Date of Consultation: THURSDAY, *AUGUST 6, 2015*
   Consulting Physician: Dr. Philip Sawyer, M.D.
   Patient: Elizabeth Percy
   Identification: Patient is a 20-year-old female.
   Presenting Complaint(s): Grandiose Delusional
Disorder
   History of Present Illness: Delusional behavior
reported at age 7.
   Current Medications: None
   Personal History: Single. No children. No significant
other. No immediate family.
   Family History: Unknown
   Mental Status Examination: Called patient in for
follow-up to yesterday's breakthrough. Patient described
another delusional experience derived from text she read
before going to bed. In her delusion, she was able to
ascertain that sorcery or wizardry is not real. This
revelation leads her to doubt her entire delusional
existence.

Laboratory Data: N/A

Diagnosis:

Axis I: Grandiose Delusional Disorder

Axis II: Deferred

Axis III: Sleep Study pending; could discover physiological ailment

Axis IV: Patient is hosting dinner with neighbor. Patient has agreed to attend a summer concert at the park next Tuesday evening.

Axis V: Current Global Assessment of Functioning rated at 71-80. Patient is seeking help to eradicate delusions.

Recommendation and Plan: Will continue out-patient psychotherapy once a week. Sleep study has been scheduled. Delusions have always presented as a separate existence only during patient's sleeping hours. Will seek experts in dream analysis.

Psychiatric Assessment - E. Percy 2015-08-07

PSYCHIATRIC ASSESSMENT
From the office of Dr. Philip Sawyer

Date of Consultation: FRIDAY, *AUGUST 7, 2015*
   Consulting Physician: Dr. Philip Sawyer, M.D.
   Patient: Elizabeth Percy
   Identification: Patient is a 20-year-old female.
   Presenting Complaint(s): Grandiose Delusional
Disorder
   History of Present Illness: Delusional behavior
reported at age 7.
   Current Medications: None
   Personal History: Single. No children. No significant
other. No immediate family.
   Family History: Unknown
   Mental Status Examination: Patient was waiting for
me in the parking lot in a disheveled state. Patient was
bleeding from a cut on her hand she received from the
broken shards of a mirror she punched out of anger. The
cut is superficial and will not require stitches. She was
wearing pajamas, no shoes and hair was unkempt.
Patient experienced shock and anger from the previous

108

evening's dream/delusion. In her delusion, she discovered her other life belongs to her twin sister, her lover is her half-brother, and her father is not a nobleman but instead a sorcerer. She was most disturbed by the "revelation" of her half-brother. In her delusions, she had experienced passion and some romantic intimacy with this character. Her mind is likely creating the taboo of incest and change of paternity to ease the transition away from the delusional state. She is choosing to see the delusions as a life belonging to someone else (her twin).

Laboratory Data: N/A

Diagnosis:

Axis I: Grandiose Delusional Disorder

Axis II: Deferred

Axis III: Pending sleep study

Axis IV: High Stress factors contributing from delusional state; i.e. incest and change of paternity (see Mental Status Examination notes).

Axis V: Current Global Assessment of Functioning rated at 11-20. Evidence of danger to self or could bring harm to others involuntarily.

Recommendation and Plan: Patient may require additional sessions on an "as needed" basis during this transitional stage. Patient is required to check in daily while she is experiencing heightened emotional state. The delusions are currently confined to her sleep state. Medication is not required so long as interactions with characters do not reveal to her in waking hours. Prognosis is optimistic that patient is separating her life from that of her delusions.

Appendix

Liz's Time Zone Difference Chart

Marysville, California		Hadleigh, Suffolk, England	
1PM		9PM	
2PM		10PM	
3PM		11PM	
4PM		12AM	Asleep in
5PM		1AM	Hadleigh
6PM		2AM	
7PM		3AM	
8PM		4AM	
9PM		5AM	
10PM		6AM	
11PM		7AM	
12AM		8AM	
1AM	Asleep in	9AM	
2AM	Marysville	10AM	
3AM		11AM	
4AM		12PM	
5AM		1PM	
6AM		2PM	
7AM		3PM	
8AM		4PM	
9AM	Extra	5PM	Extra
10AM	Time	6PM	Time
11AM		7PM	
12PM		8PM	

Note from Author

Spoiler Alert: Changing Realms Plot and Ending

May 20, 2022

Dear Reader,

Thank you so much for taking the time to read my short novella, Changing Realms. I cannot believe it has been seven years since I wrote this story! It seems the perception of time can be tricky in several ways. Whether the years go by so slowly during a pandemic, or you encapsulate a wonderful day by a stream near the south border in the blink of an eye.

When I originally published this story, I was a relatively new author excited by the autonomy of self-publishing. I was terribly impatient to get this story out in the world, and I feel I cut a few corners. As the years went by, I continued to write. I had to pause my storytelling for a little while to make some money in the real world. I longed to return to my author self, and here I am. Feeling fortunate to return to my characters, settings, and trying to sneak in as many twists as I can along the way.

While working on new material, I stopped to look at my backlog. Changing Realms differs from my usual science/technology fare, but still has the stamp of my constant curiosity about existential dilemmas. I get a lot of questions about this story because of its shorter length and open ending.

1) Will there be a continuation of Elizabeth and Liz's story?

2) Is magic real or is she delusional?

I think about this story a lot, specifically these questions. I want to dig deeper into the Changing Realms universe. I hope I have time to circle back to it someday. I have so many stories I want to share with you, but this one was tugging at me the past few months, so I had to stop and give it some attention.

Because I was a novice when I wrote it (not that I see myself as a master of the trade now), and I have collected so many new resources to help me with the editing process, I pulled out the manuscript and took it through a line by line edit. The story did not change, but the readability is more polished, and I am embarrassed to admit there were a few grammatical errors.

While I was reviewing the story line by line, I fell in love with this universe again. I have a few works in line ahead of it, but I can see myself coming back to this story. So answering the first question, yes, I hope to produce a continuation of the Changing Realms universe in the future.

As for the second question. Is magic real, or is she delusional? According to my daydreams, the answer is yes, magic is real! I would love so much to explore how Matias's magic works. Can he conjure a spell to un-link

Liz and Elizabeth's consciousnesses? How does his magic work? Will Liz inherit powers, or is it all physics science the world has yet to figure out?

I would love to hear your thoughts! I encourage you to e-mail me at shona@shonabradbury.com. To follow the latest news about my work go to www.shonabradbury.com.

Always grateful,
Shona Bradbury